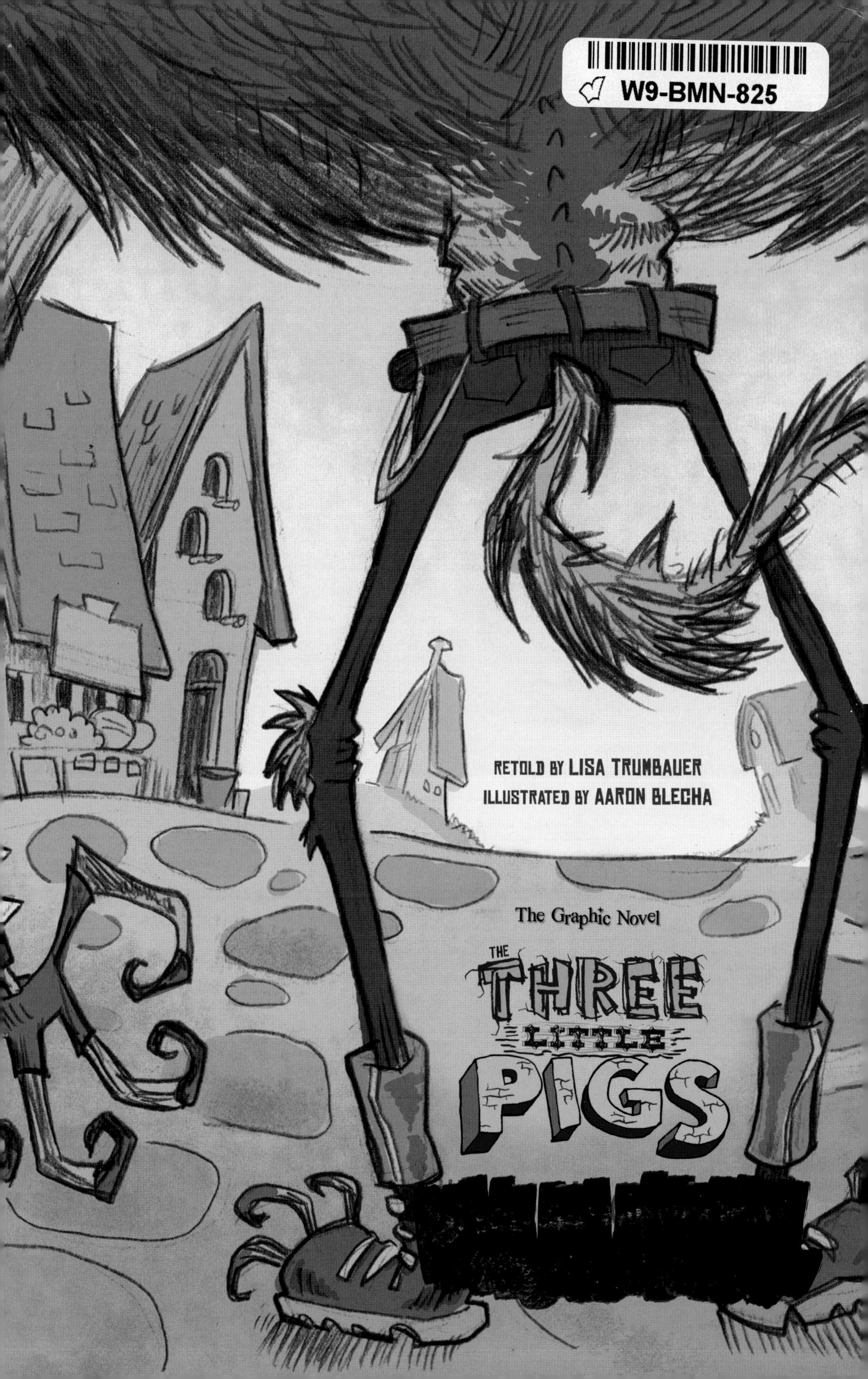
RETOLD BY LISA TRUMBAUER
ILLUSTRATED BY AARON BLECHA
The Graphic Novel
THE THREE LITTLE PIGS
[redacted]

Graphic Spin is published by Stone Arch Books,
A Capstone Imprint
151 Good Counsel Drive, P.O. Box 669
Mankato, Minnesota 56002
www.capstonepub.com

Library of Congress Cataloging-in-Publication Data
Trumbauer, Lisa, 1963-
     The Three Little Pigs / by Lisa Trumbauer; illustrated by Aaron Blecha.
     p. cm. — (Graphic Spin)
     ISBN 978-1-4342-1195-8 (library binding)
     ISBN 978-1-4342-1395-2 (pbk.)
     1. Graphic novels. [1. Graphic novels. 2. Folkore. 3. Pigs—Folklore.] I. Blecha, Aaron, ill.
II. Three little pigs. English. III. Title.
PZ7.7.T78Th 2009
741.5'973—dc22   2008032050

Summary: When their mother sends them packing, the Three Little Pigs are forced to build
houses of their own. They better be sturdy and strong because the Big Bad Wolf is on the prowl,
and he's ready to huff and puff his way inside. Will they survive against this hungry beast? Or
will the pigs become his next tasty treat?

Creative Director: Heather Kindseth
Designer: Bob Lentz

Printed in the United States of America in Stevens Point, Wisconsin.
022010
005712

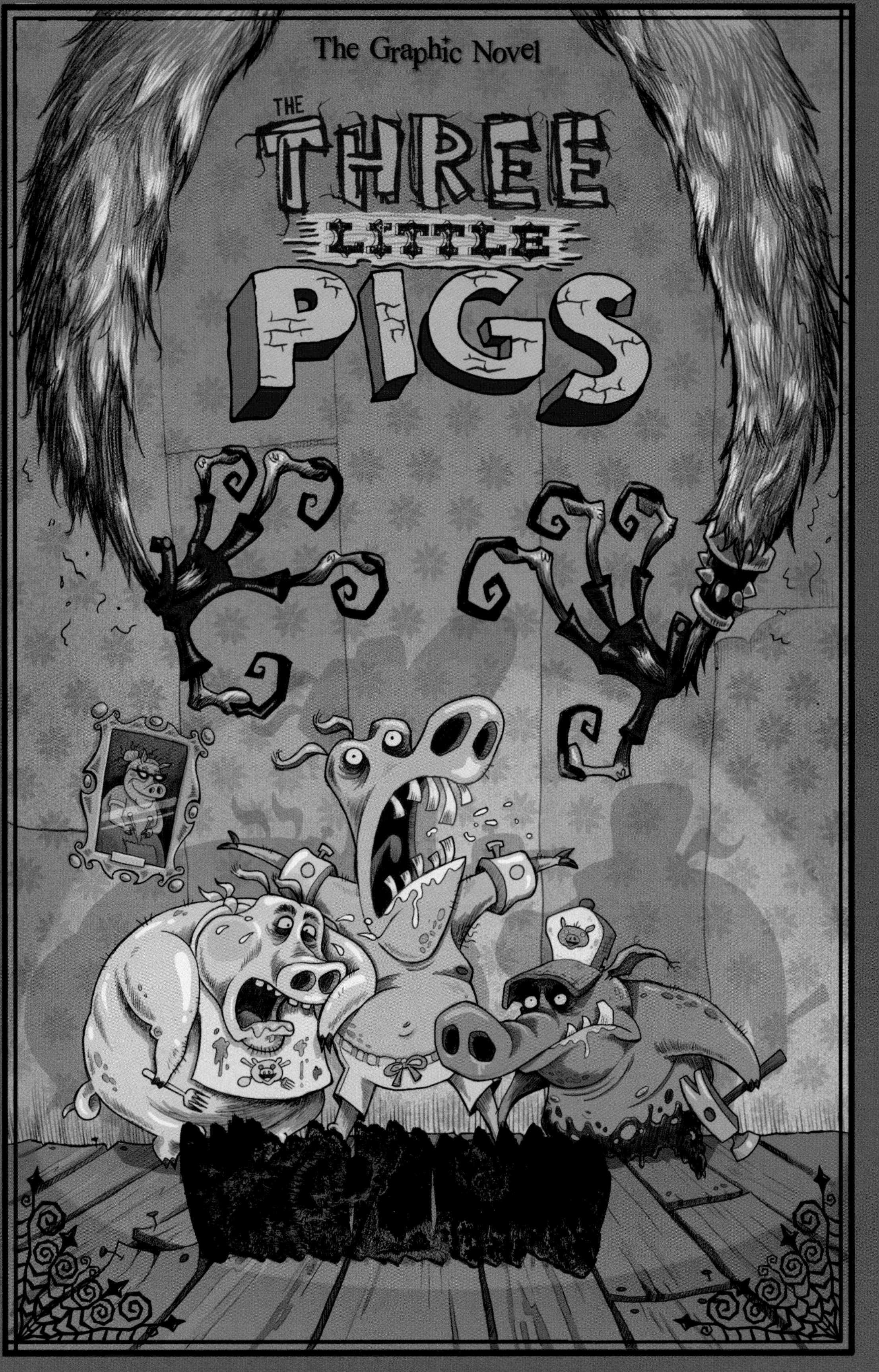
The Graphic Novel
THE THREE LITTLE PIGS

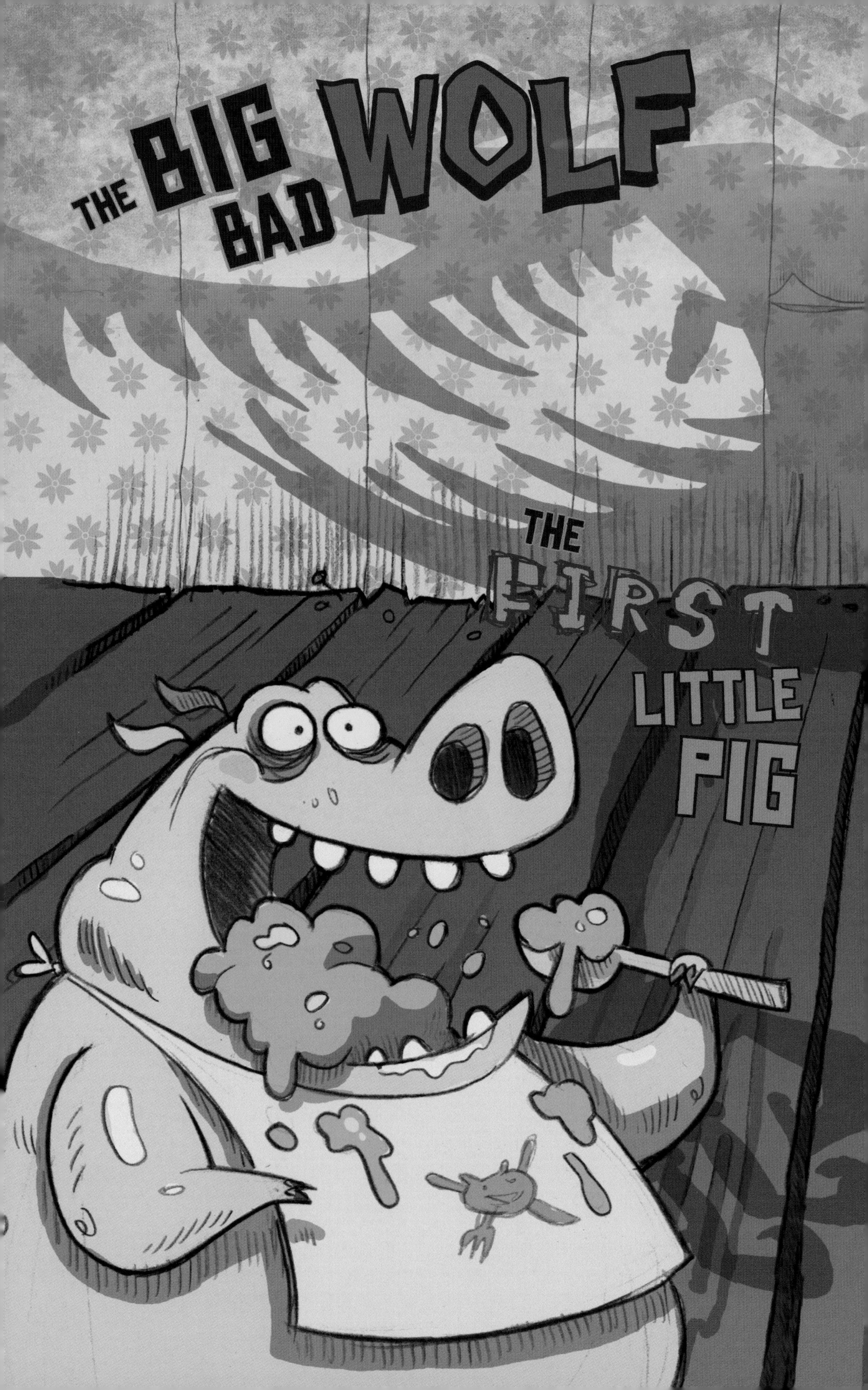
THE BIG BAD WOLF
THE FIRST LITTLE PIG

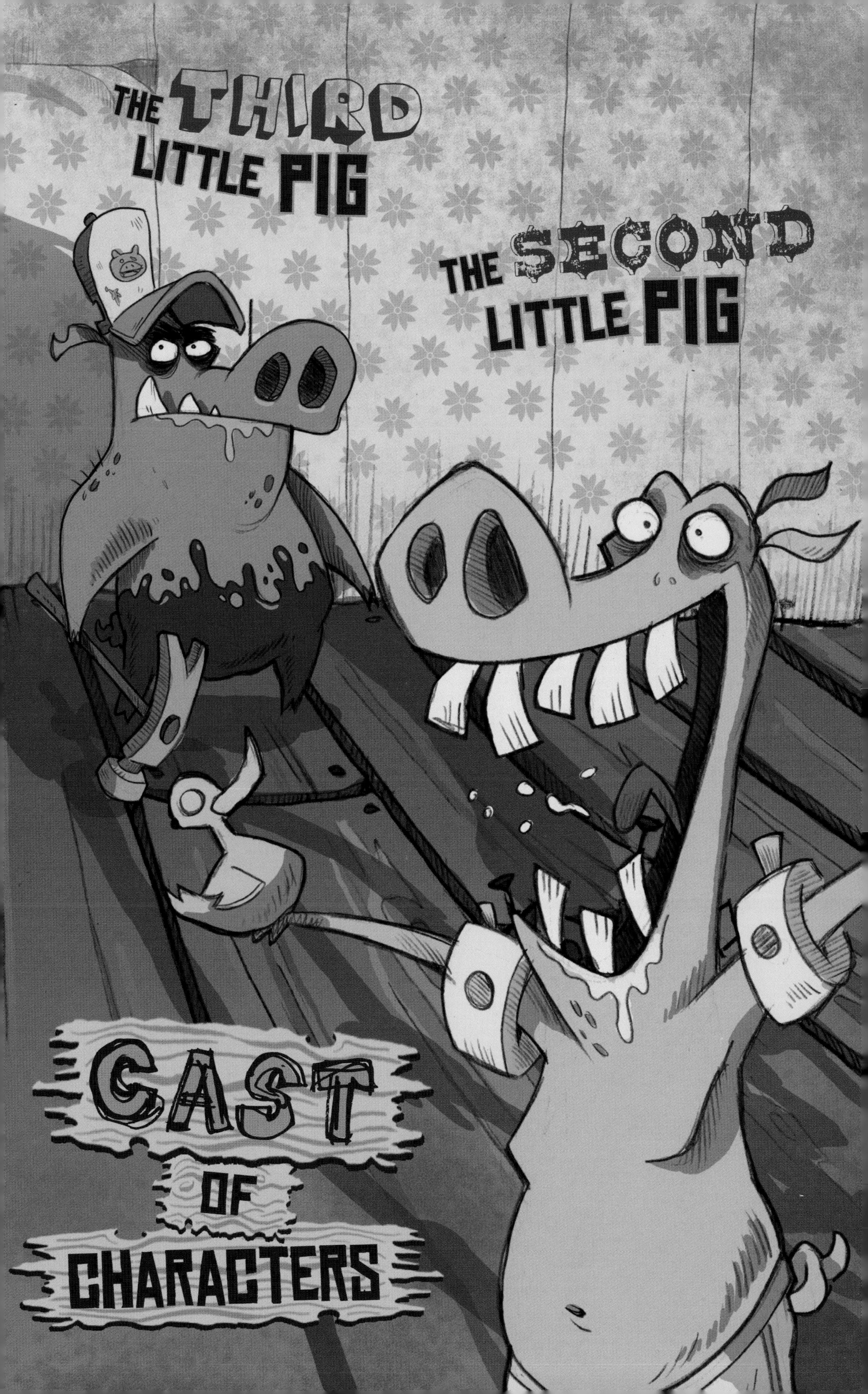
THE THIRD LITTLE PIG
THE SECOND LITTLE PIG
CAST OF CHARACTERS

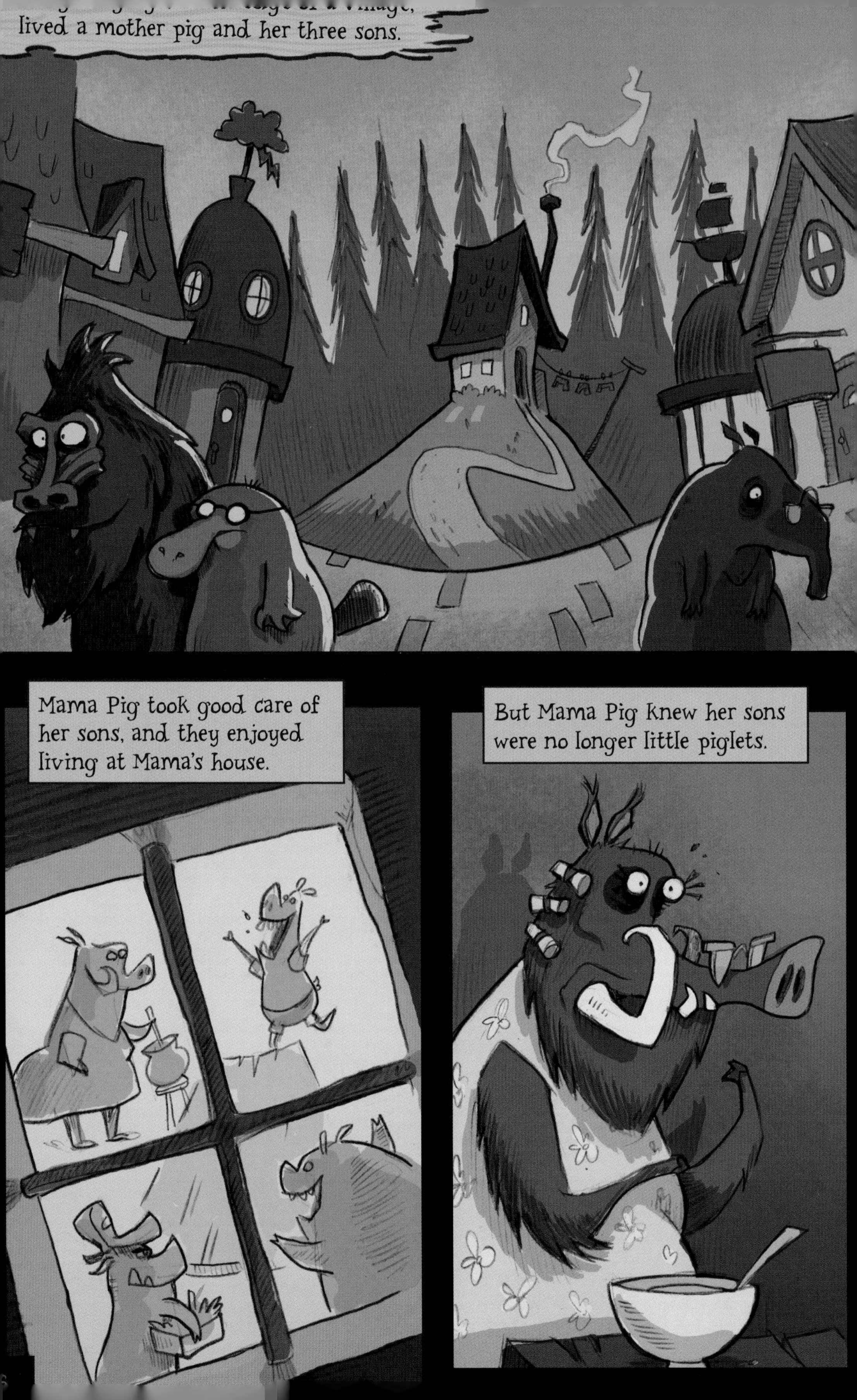
lived a mother pig and her three sons.
Mama Pig took good care of her sons, and they enjoyed living at Mama's house.
But Mama Pig knew her sons were no longer little piglets.

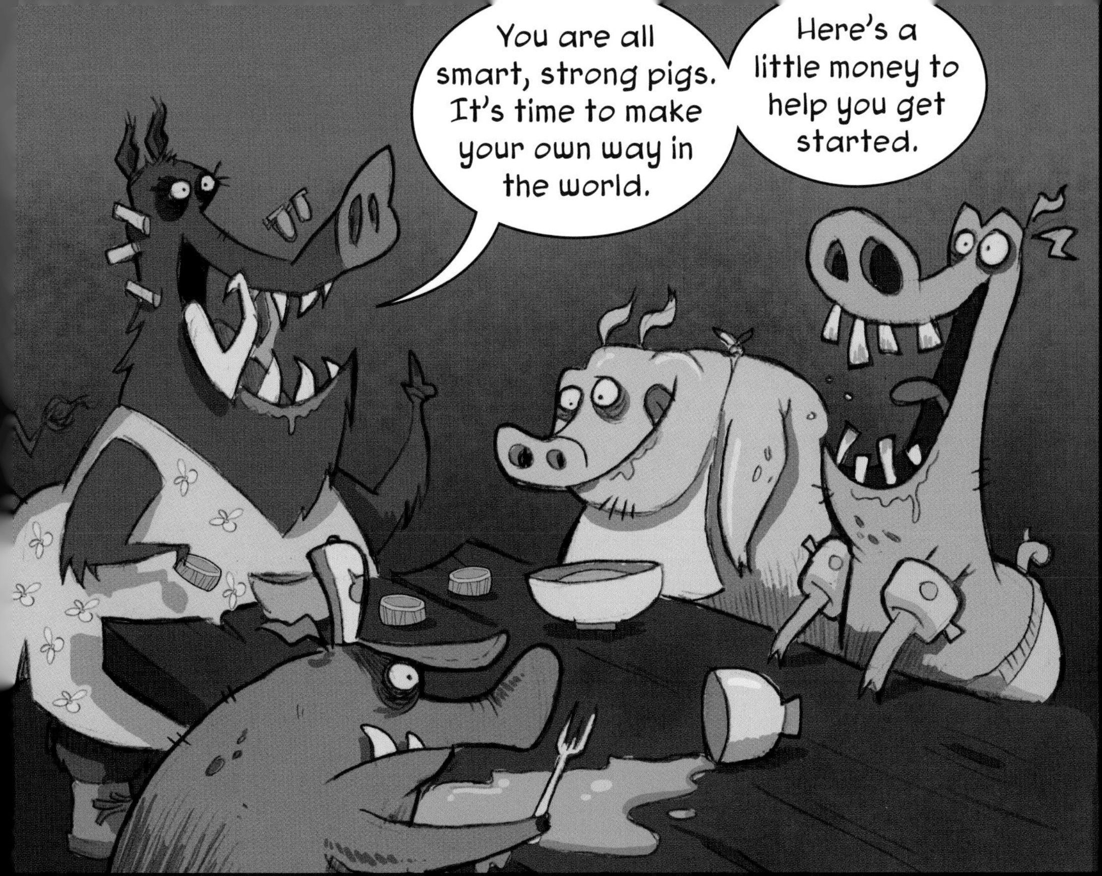
You are all smart, strong pigs. It's time to make your own way in the world.
Here's a little money to help you get started.

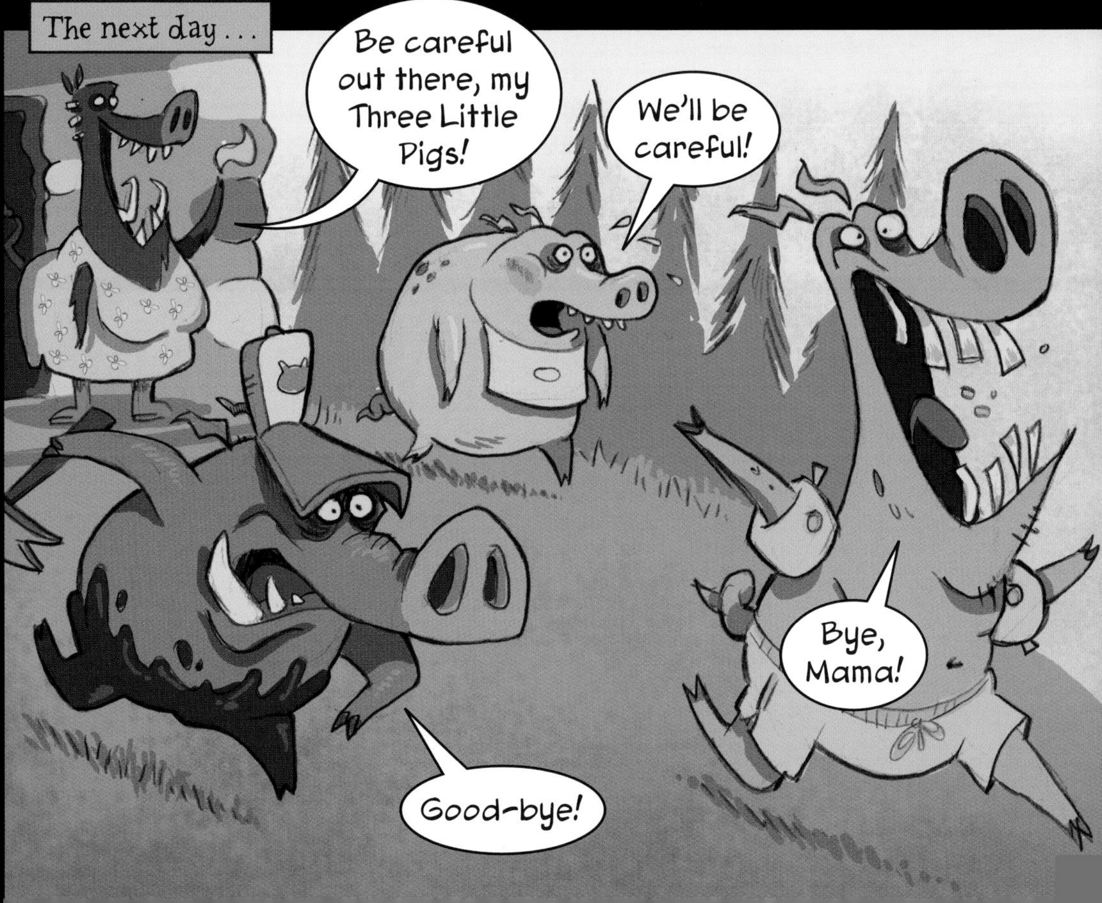
The next day . . .
Be careful out there, my Three Little Pigs!
We'll be careful!
Bye, Mama!
Good-bye!

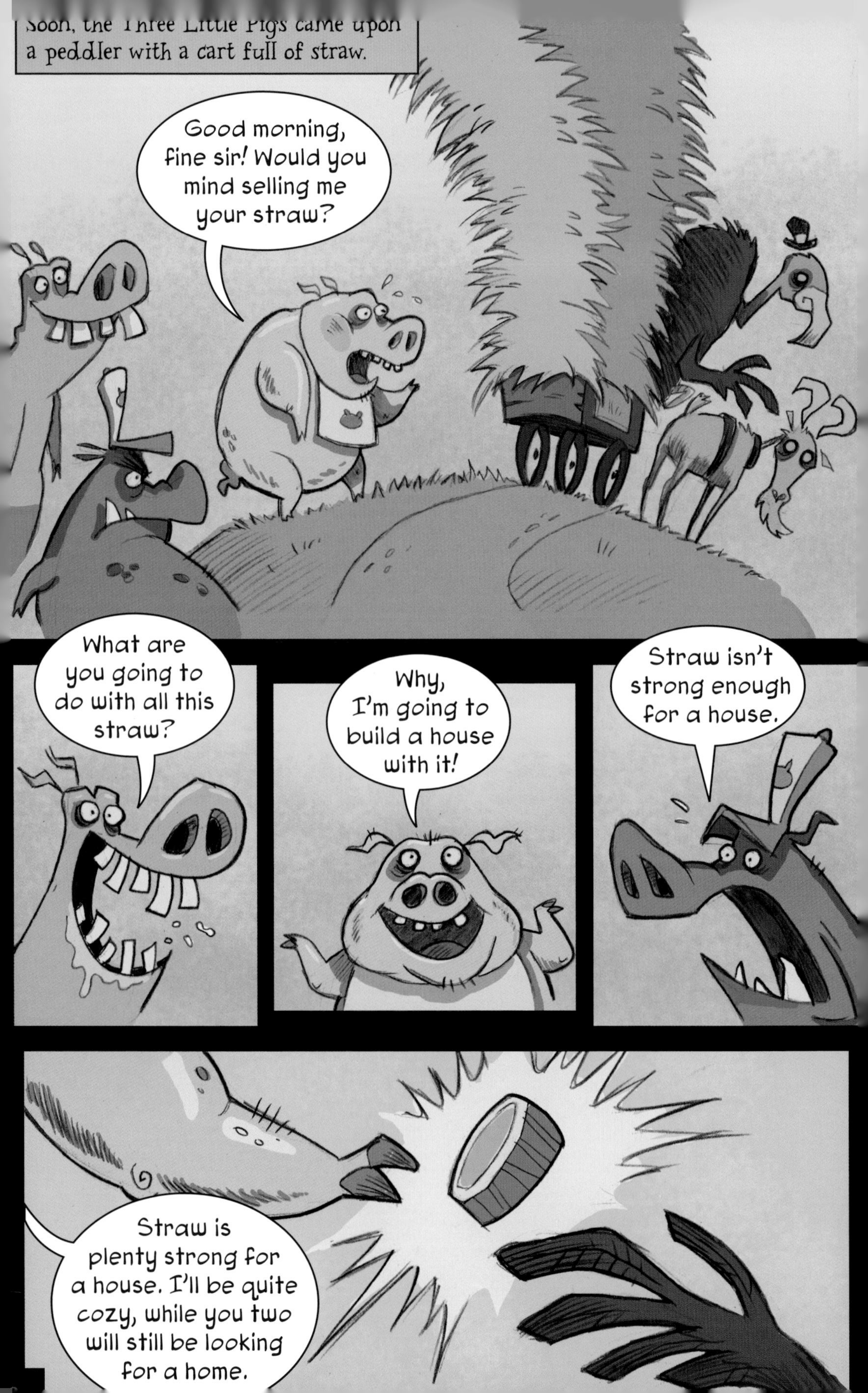
Soon, the Three Little Pigs came upon a peddler with a cart full of straw.
Good morning, fine sir! Would you mind selling me your straw?
What are you going to do with all this straw?
Why, I'm going to build a house with it!
Straw isn't strong enough for a house.
Straw is plenty strong for a house. I'll be quite cozy, while you two will still be looking for a home.

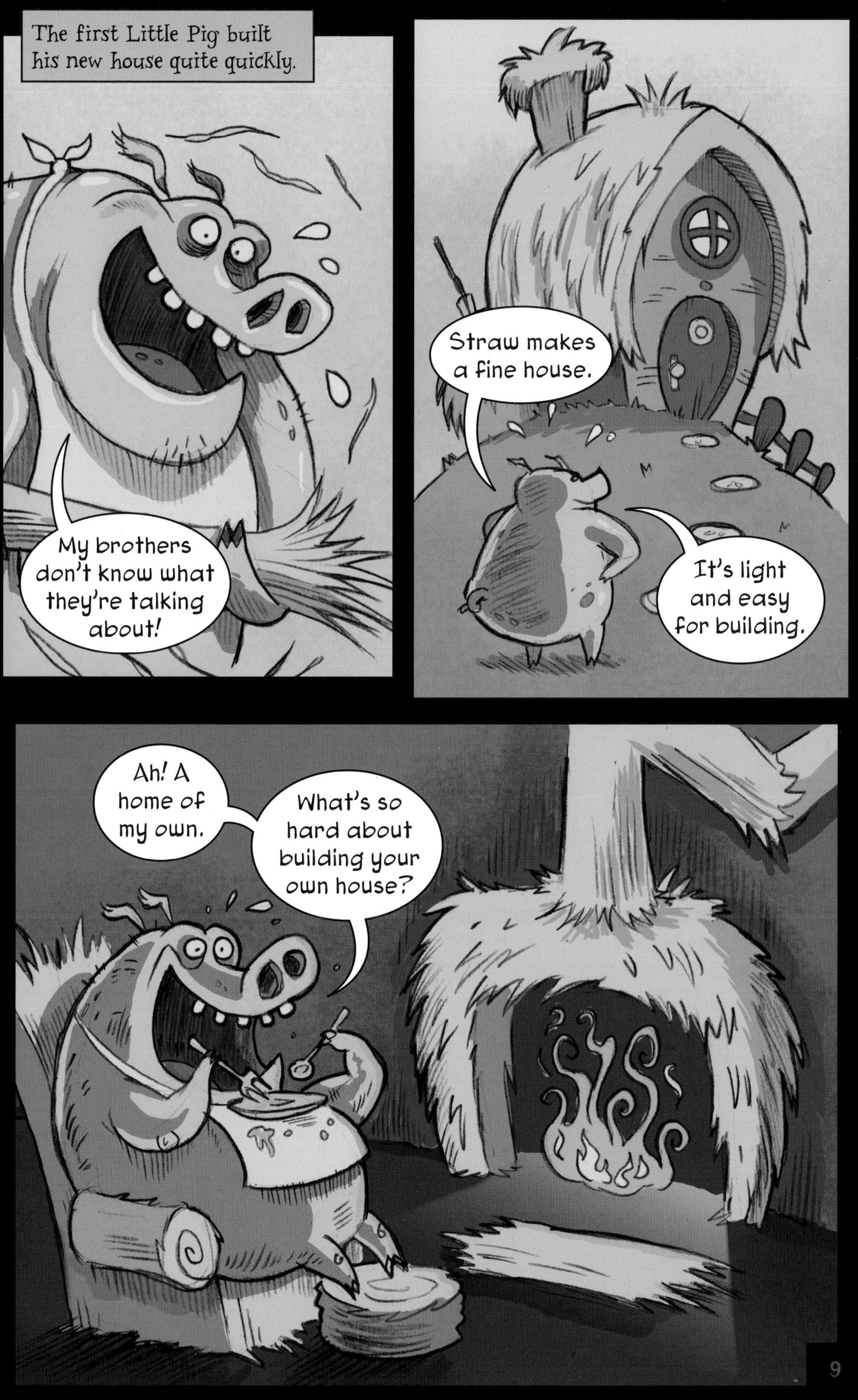
The first Little Pig built his new house quite quickly.
My brothers don't know what they're talking about!
Straw makes a fine house.
It's light and easy for building.
Ah! A home of my own.
What's so hard about building your own house?

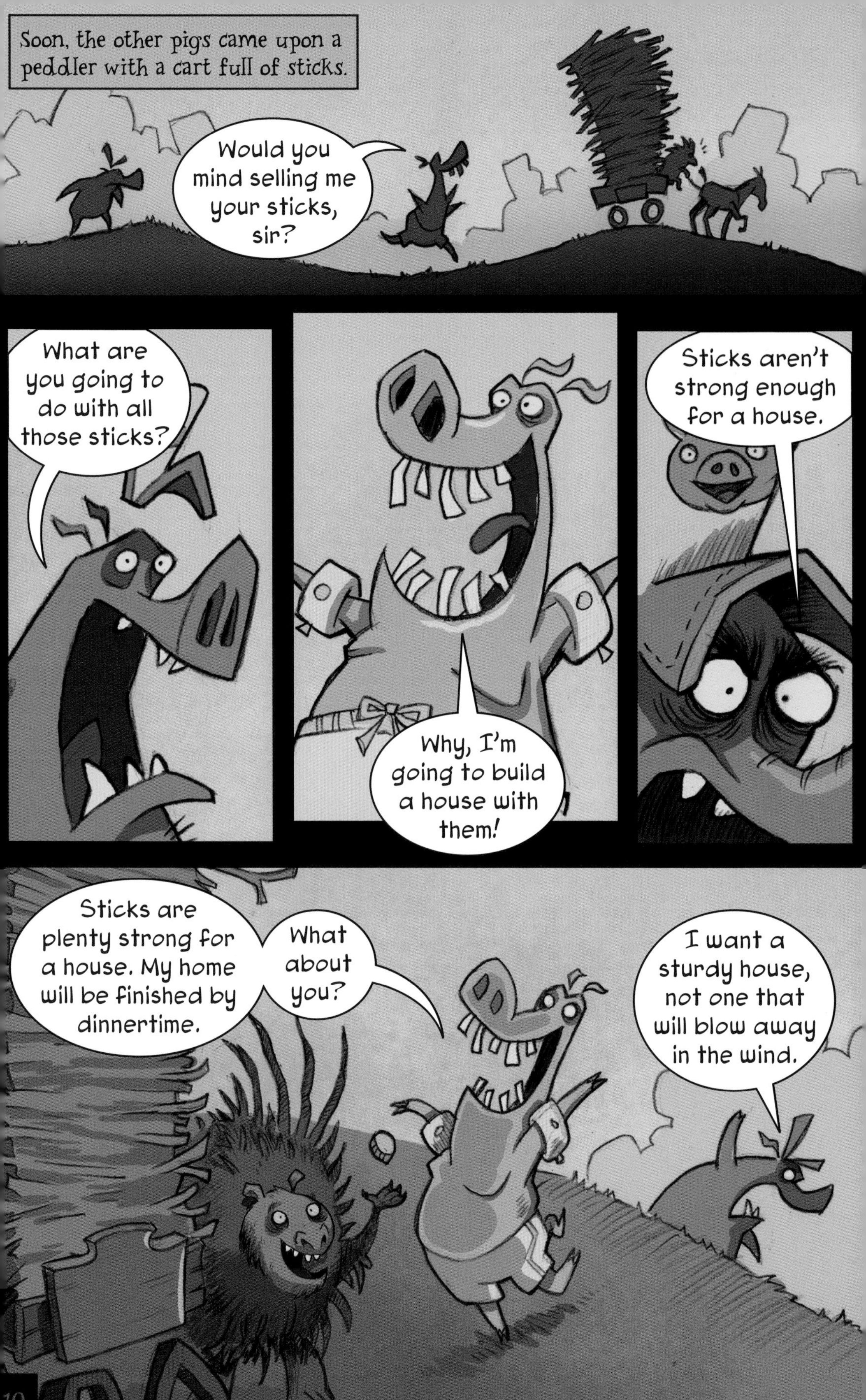
Soon, the other pigs came upon a peddler with a cart full of sticks.
Would you mind selling me your sticks, sir?
What are you going to do with all those sticks?
Why, I'm going to build a house with them!
Sticks aren't strong enough for a house.
Sticks are plenty strong for a house. My home will be finished by dinnertime.
What about you?
I want a sturdy house, not one that will blow away in the wind.

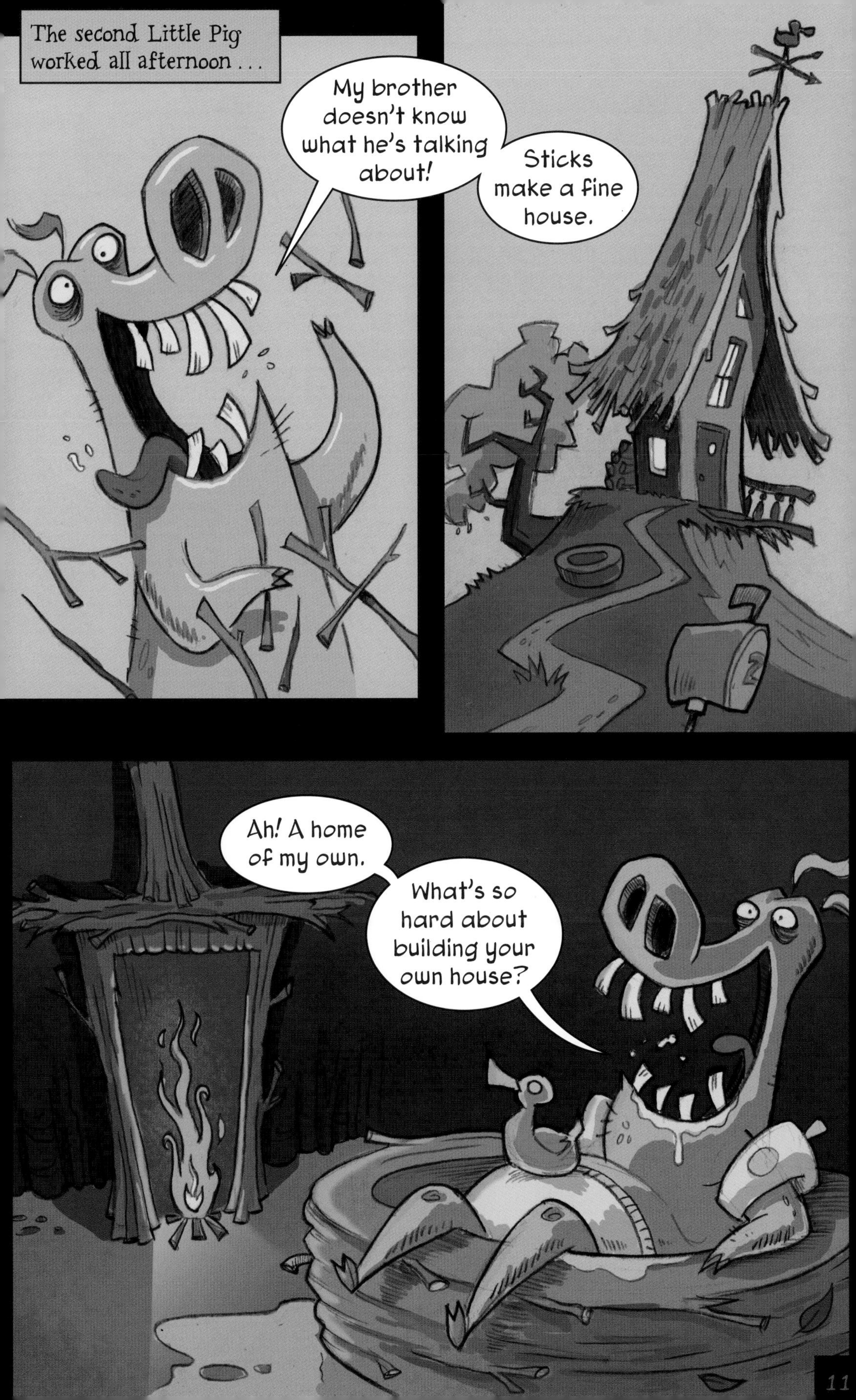
The second Little Pig worked all afternoon . . .
My brother doesn't know what he's talking about!
Sticks make a fine house.
Ah! A home of my own.
What's so hard about building your own house?

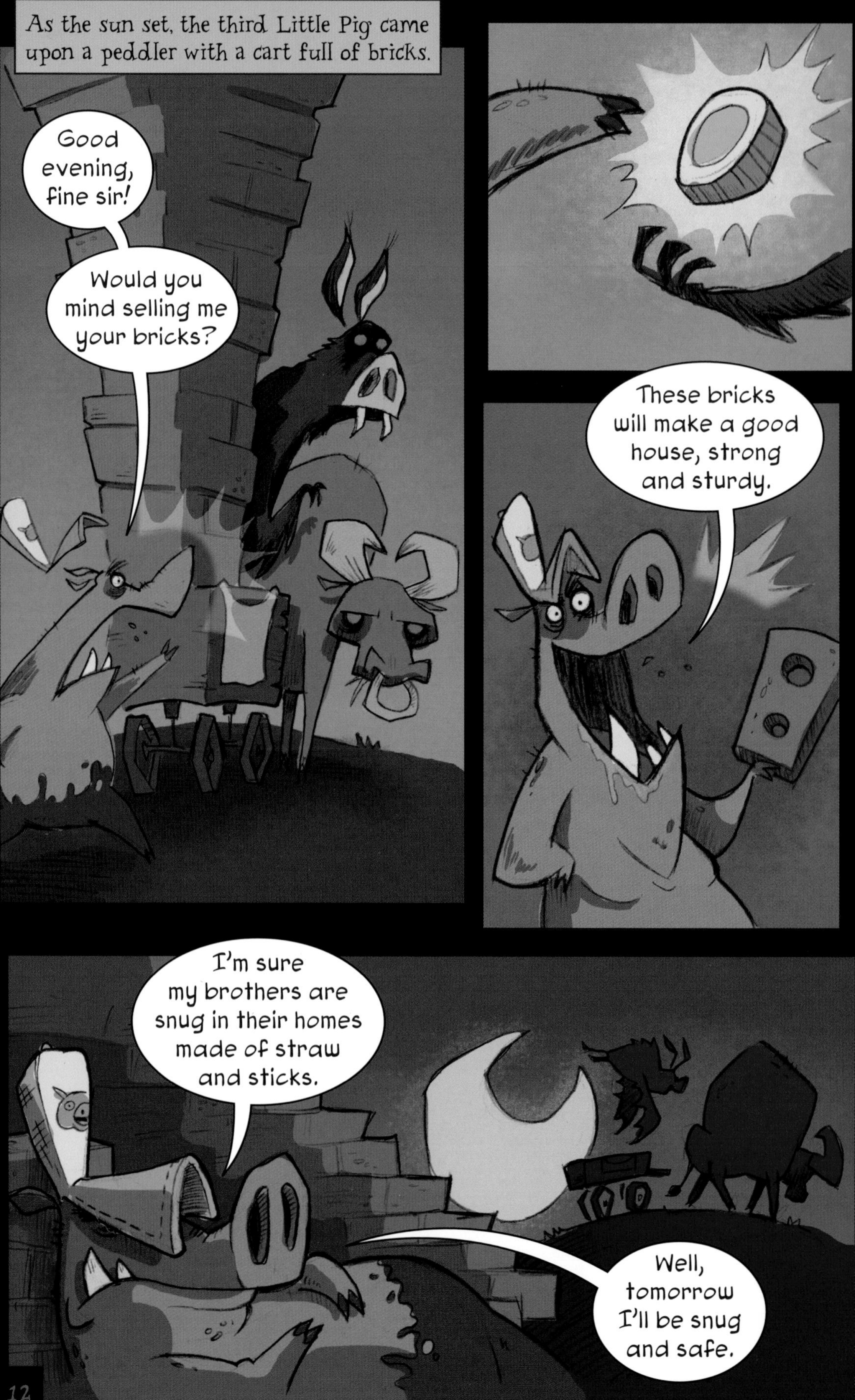
As the sun set, the third Little Pig came upon a peddler with a cart full of bricks.
Good evening, fine sir!
Would you mind selling me your bricks?
These bricks will make a good house, strong and sturdy.
I'm sure my brothers are snug in their homes made of straw and sticks.
Well, tomorrow I'll be snug and safe.

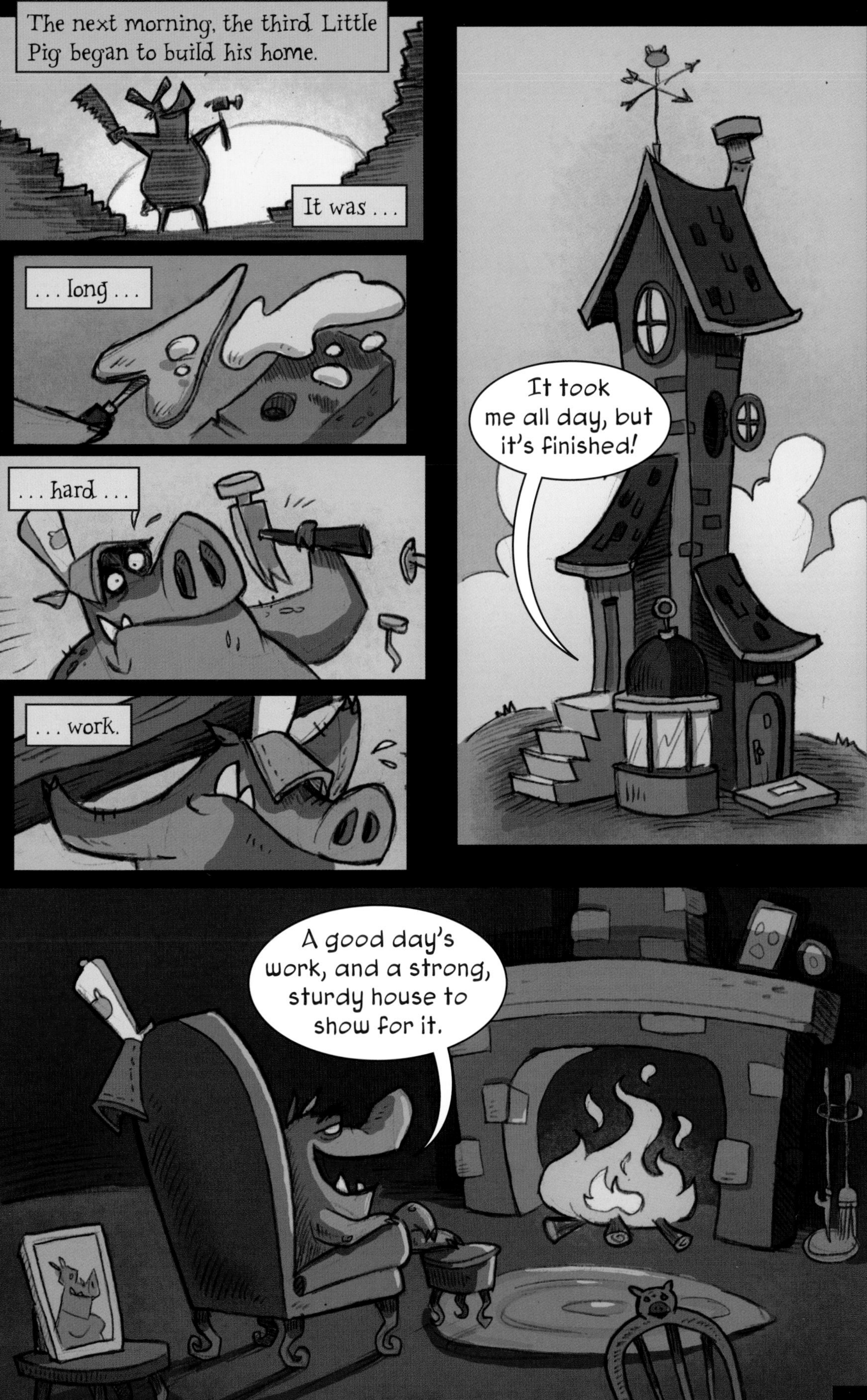
The next morning, the third Little Pig began to build his home.
It was . . .
. . . long . . .
. . . hard . . .
. . . work.
It took me all day, but it's finished!
A good day's work, and a strong, sturdy house to show for it.

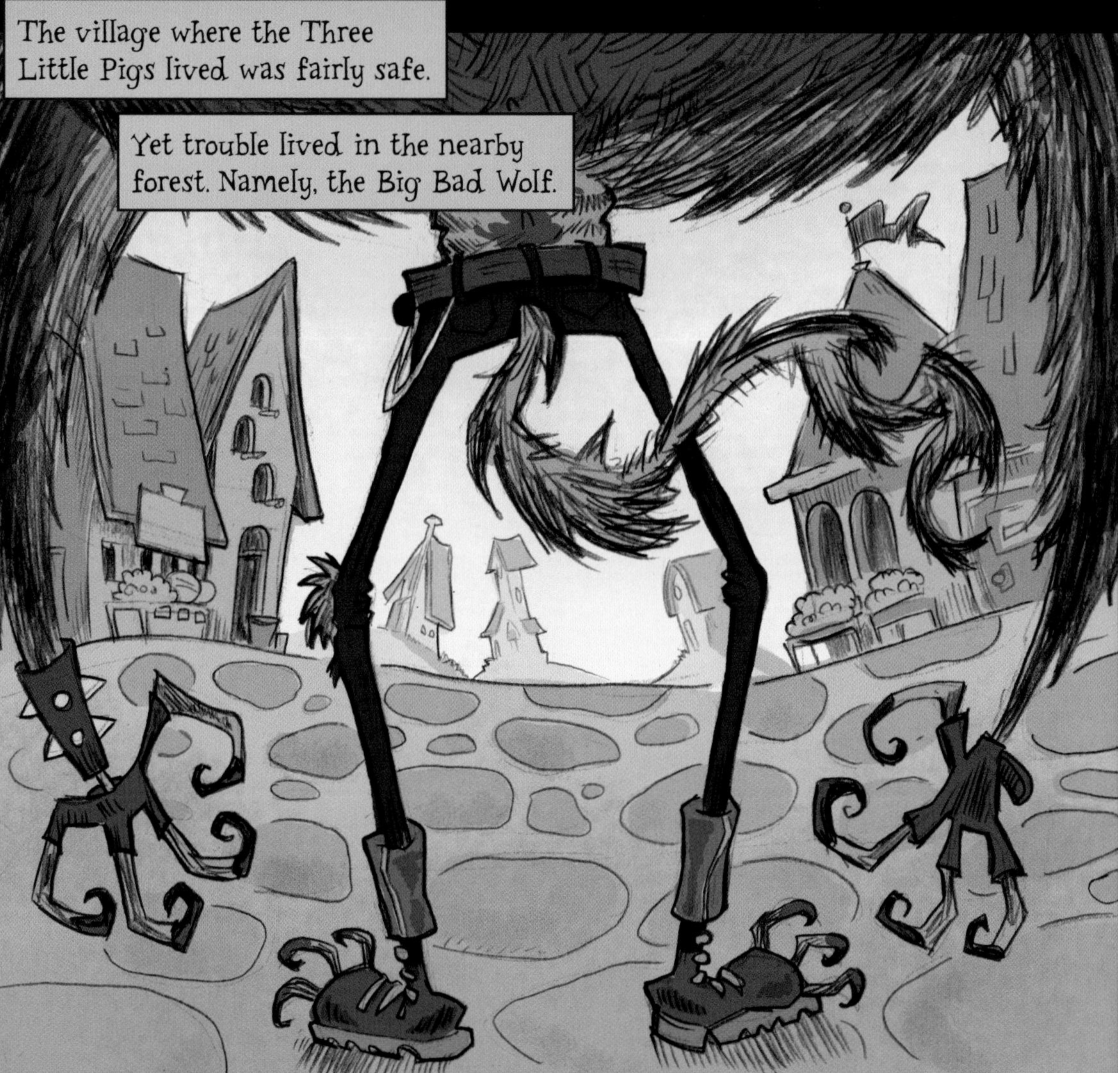
The village where the Three Little Pigs lived was fairly safe.
Yet trouble lived in the nearby forest. Namely, the Big Bad Wolf.

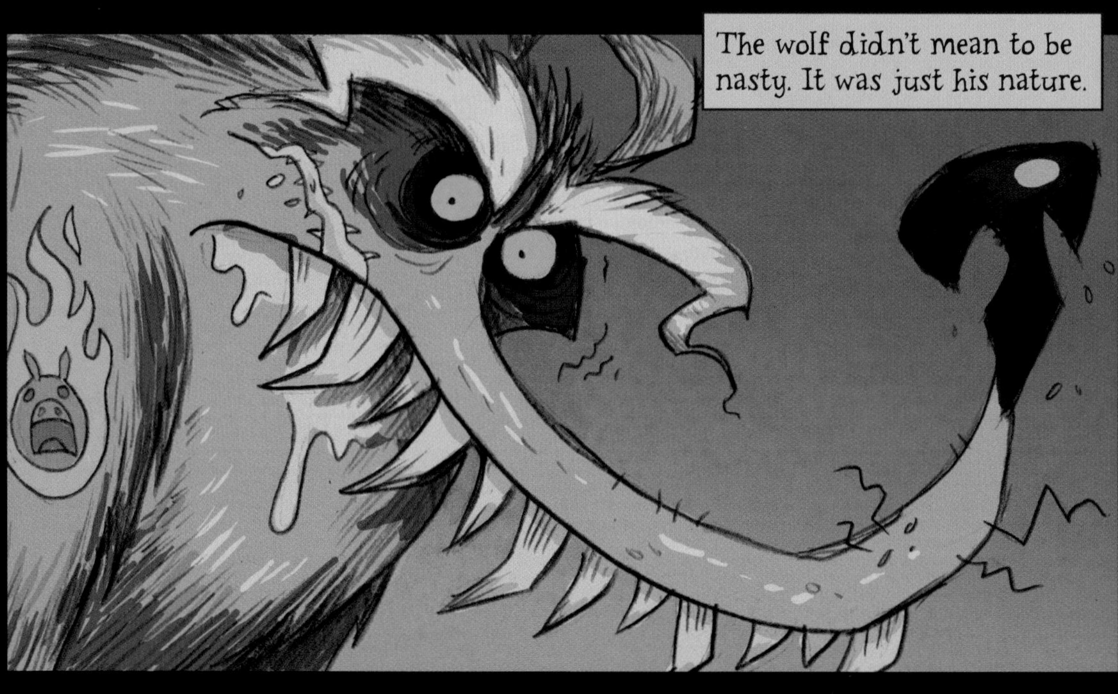
The wolf didn't mean to be nasty. It was just his nature.

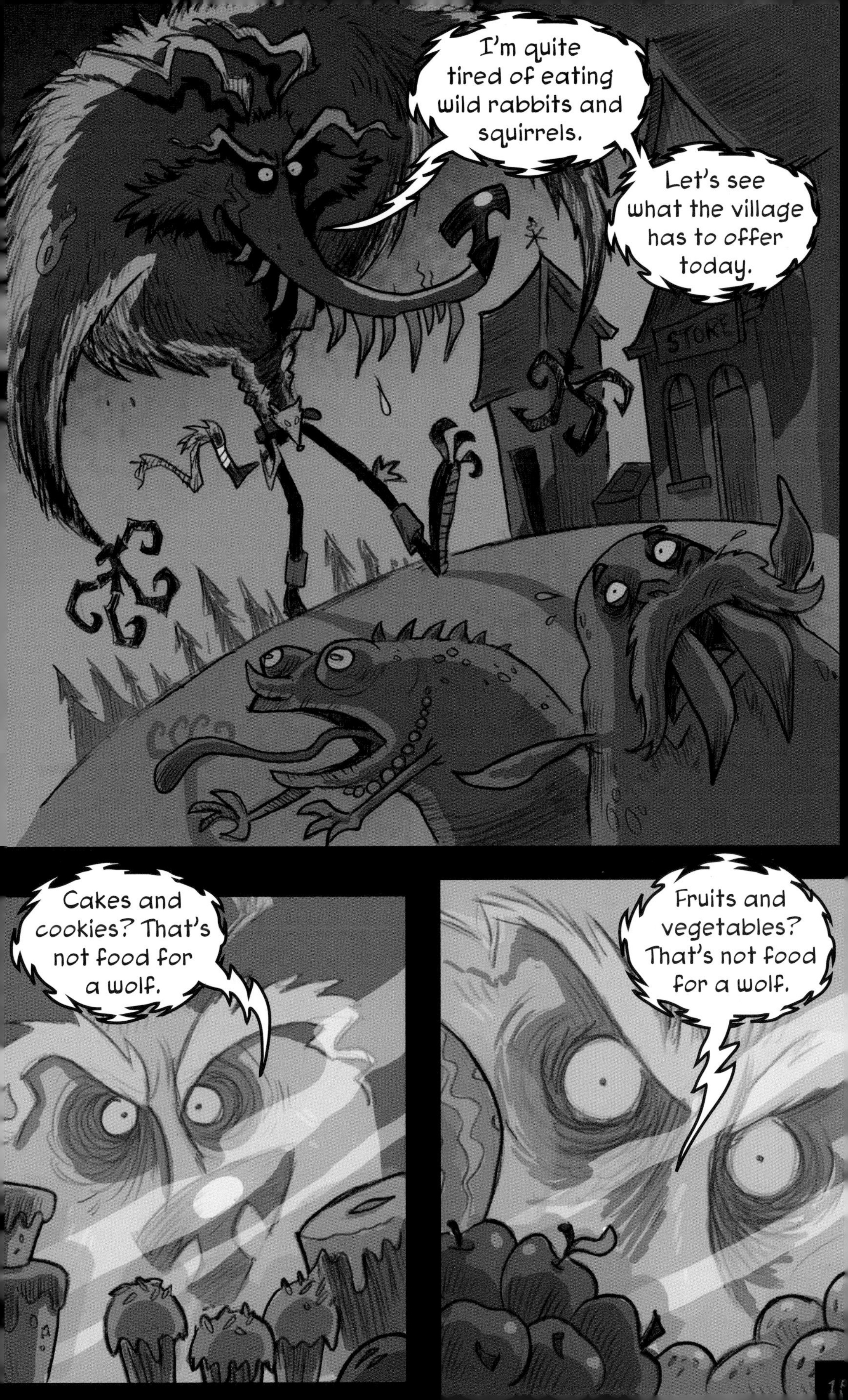
I'm quite tired of eating wild rabbits and squirrels.
Let's see what the village has to offer today.
STORE
Cakes and cookies? That's not food for a wolf.
Fruits and vegetables? That's not food for a wolf.

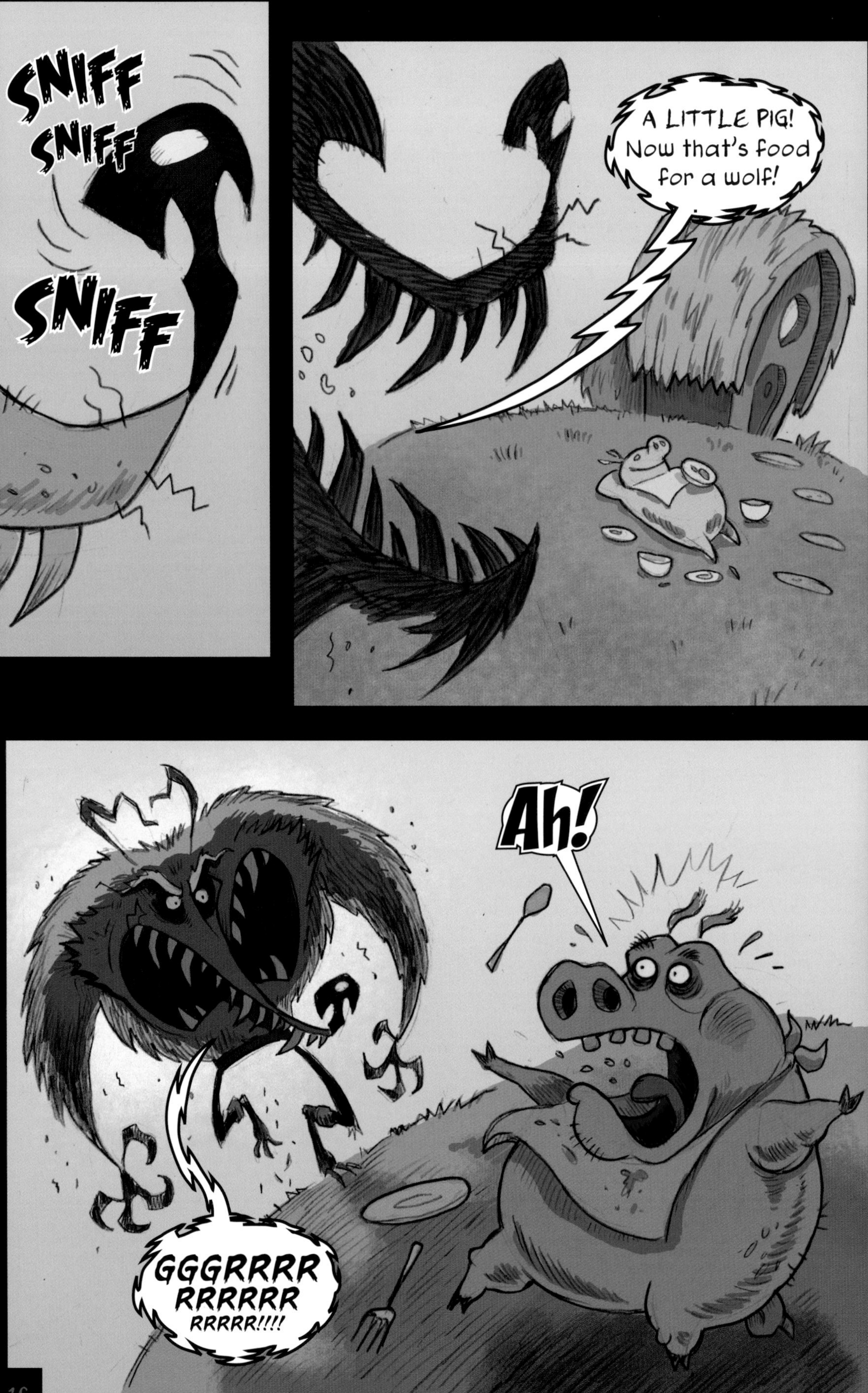
SNIFF
SNIFF
SNIFF
A LITTLE PIG! Now that's food for a wolf!
Ah!
GGGRRRR RRRRRR RRRRR!!!!

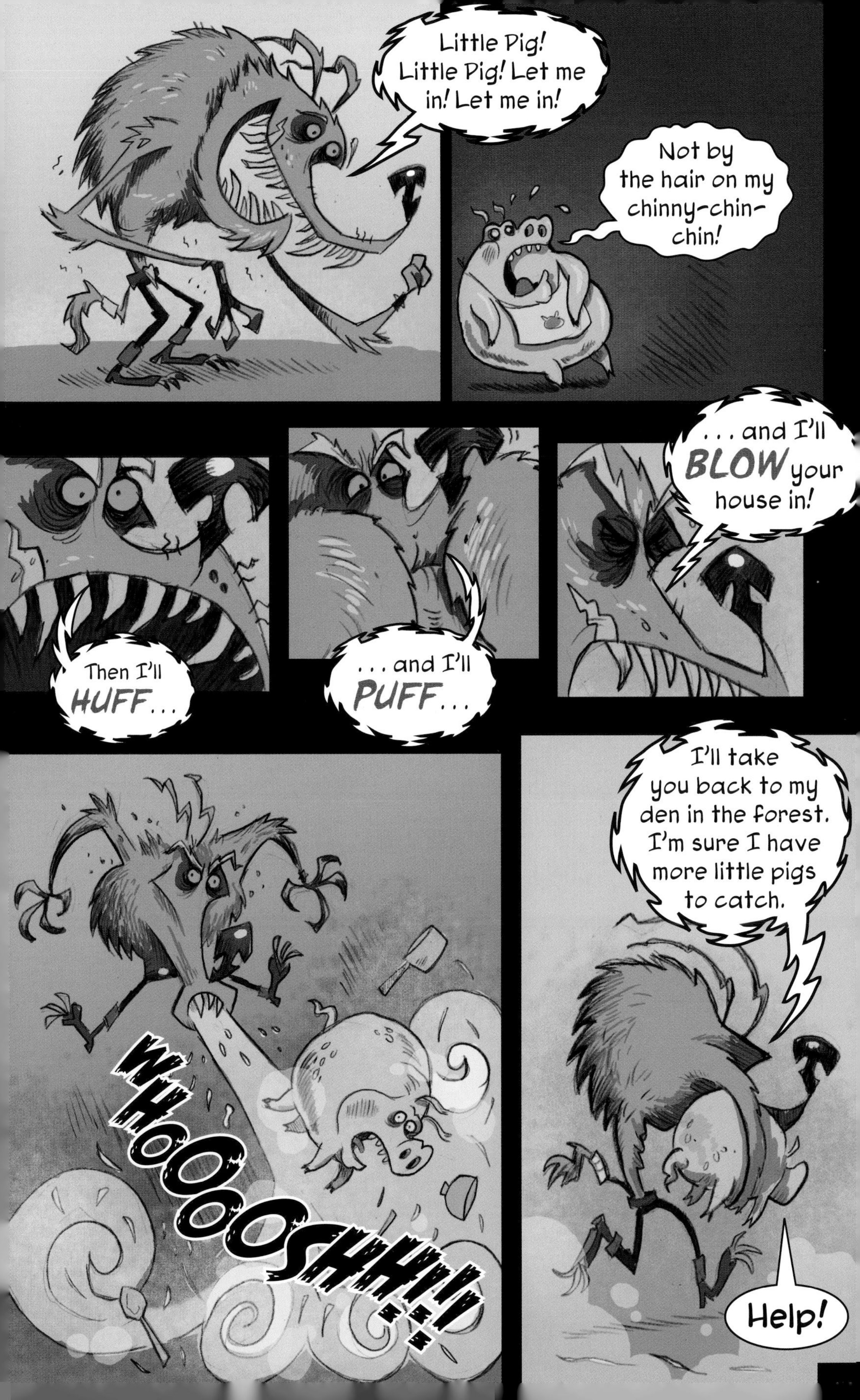
Little Pig! Little Pig! Let me in! Let me in!
Not by the hair on my chinny-chin-chin!
Then I'll HUFF...
...and I'll PUFF...
...and I'll BLOW your house in!
WHOOOOSHH!!!
I'll take you back to my den in the forest. I'm sure I have more little pigs to catch.
Help!

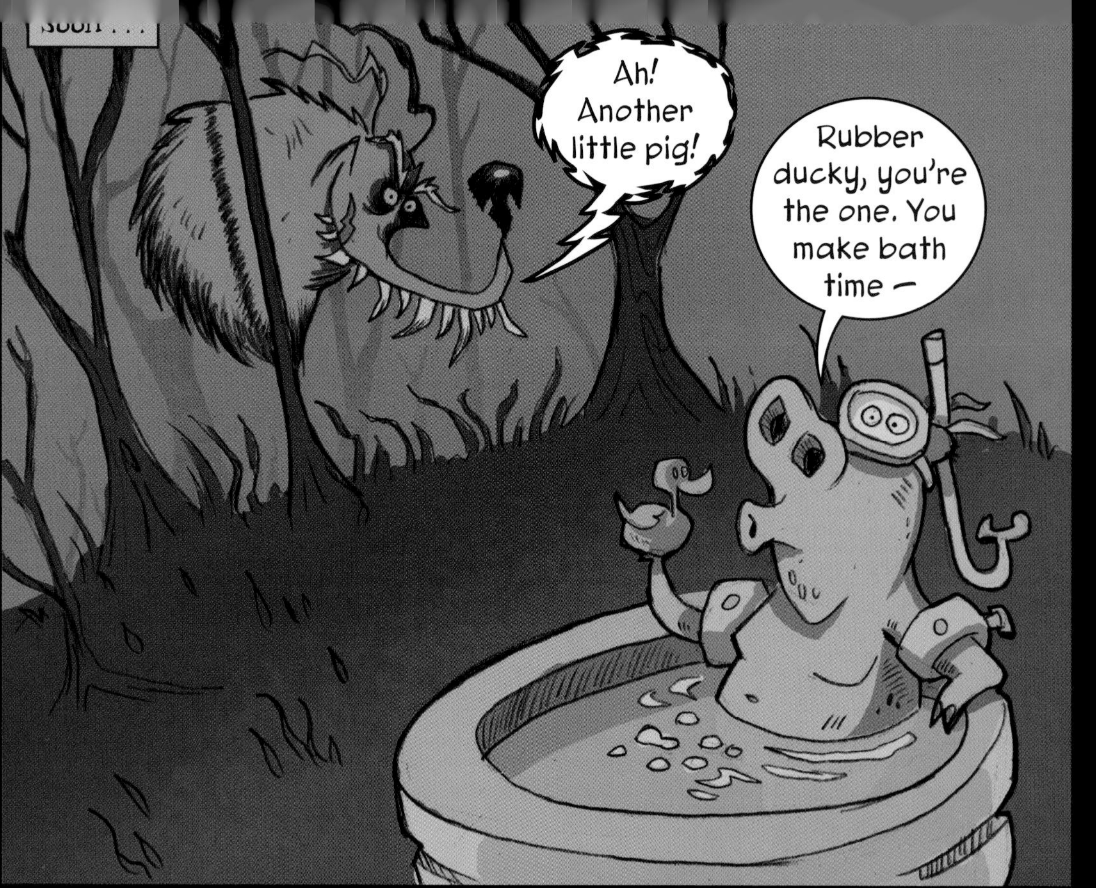
Ah! Another little pig!
Rubber ducky, you're the one. You make bath time —

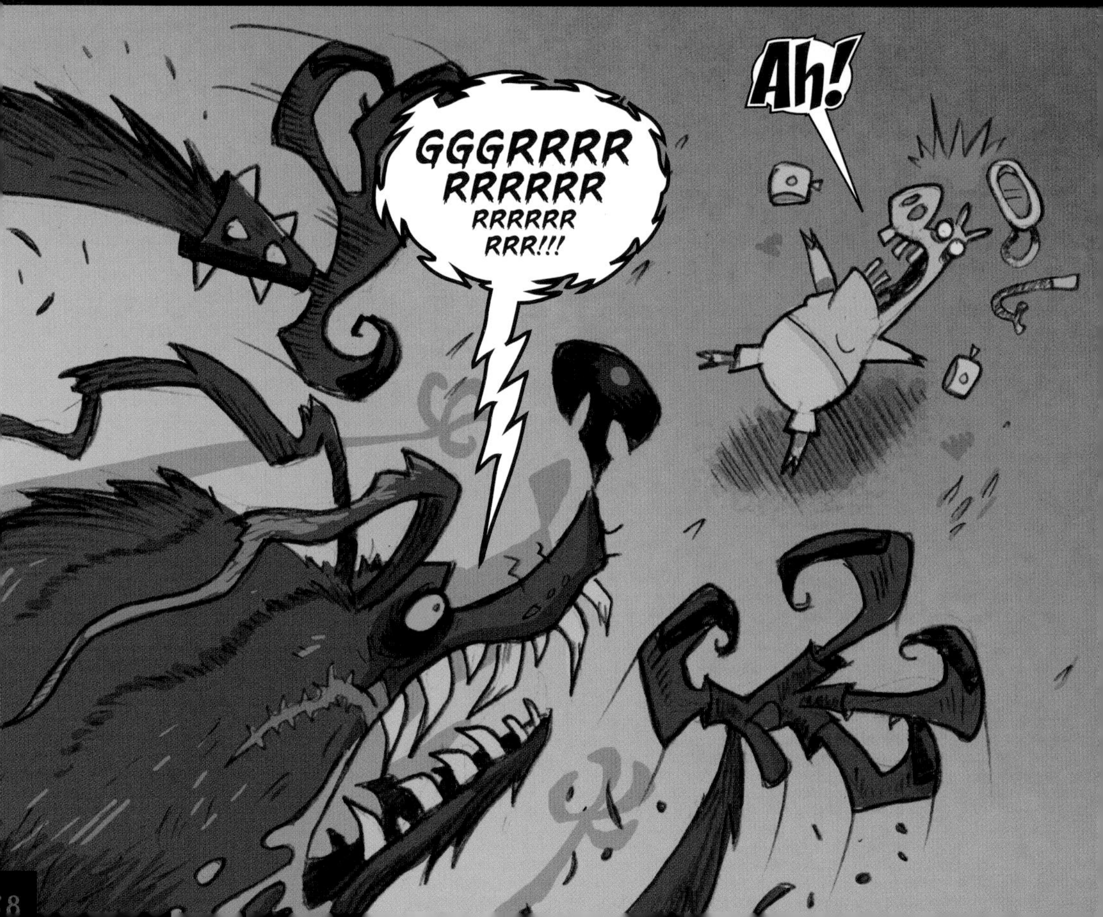
GGGRRRR RRRRRR RRRRRR RRR!!!
Ah!

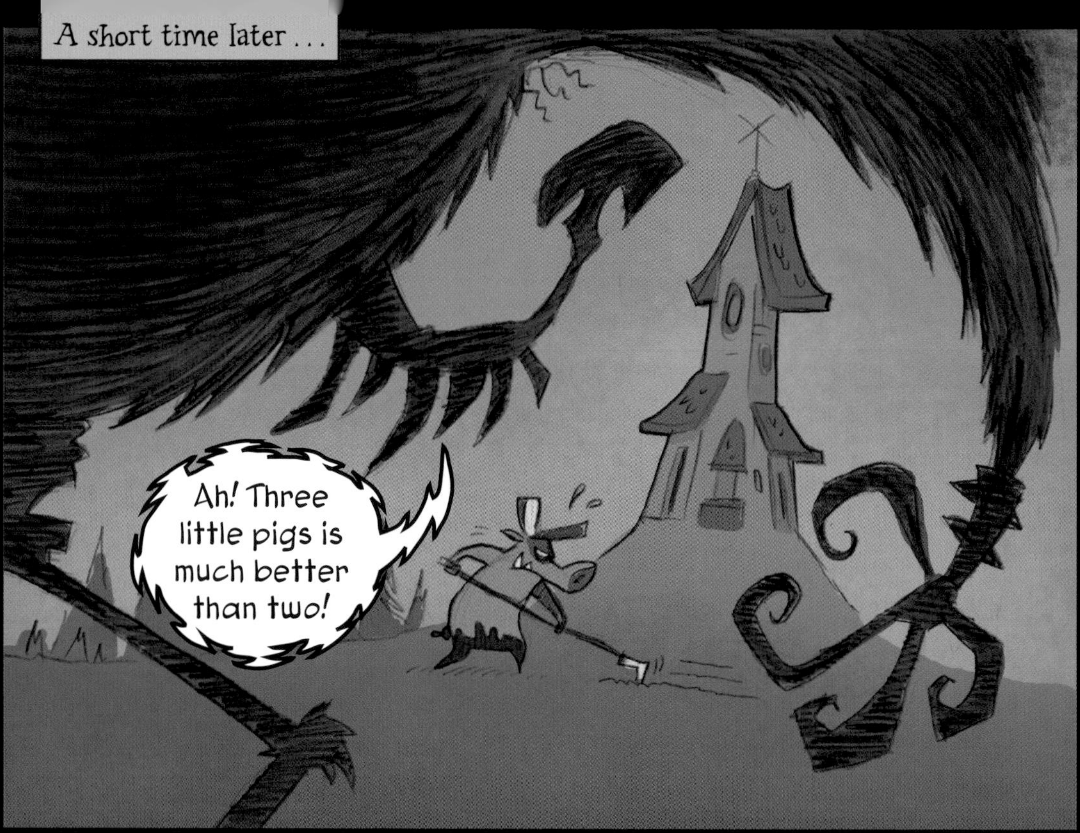
A short time later . . .
Ah! Three little pigs is much better than two!

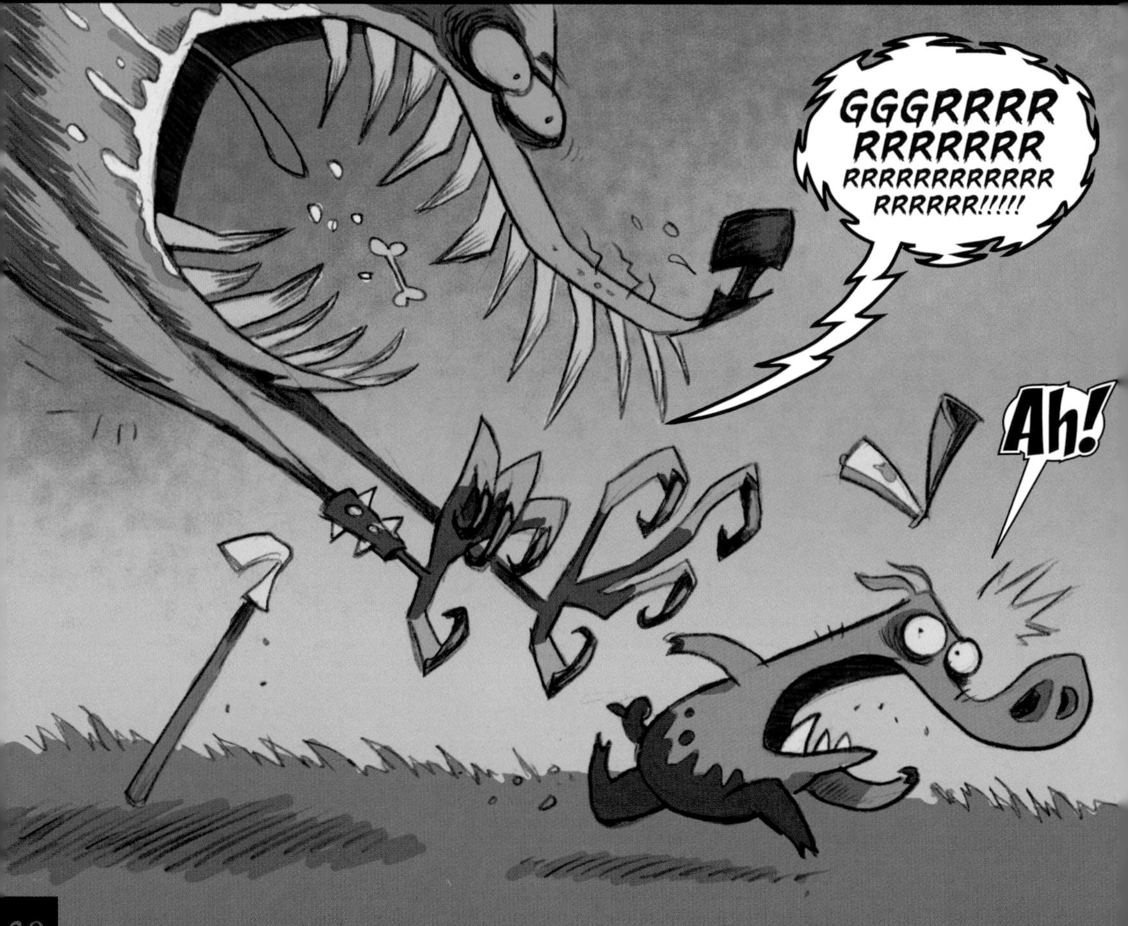
GGGRRRR RRRRRRR RRRRRRRRRRRR RRRRRR!!!!!
Ah!

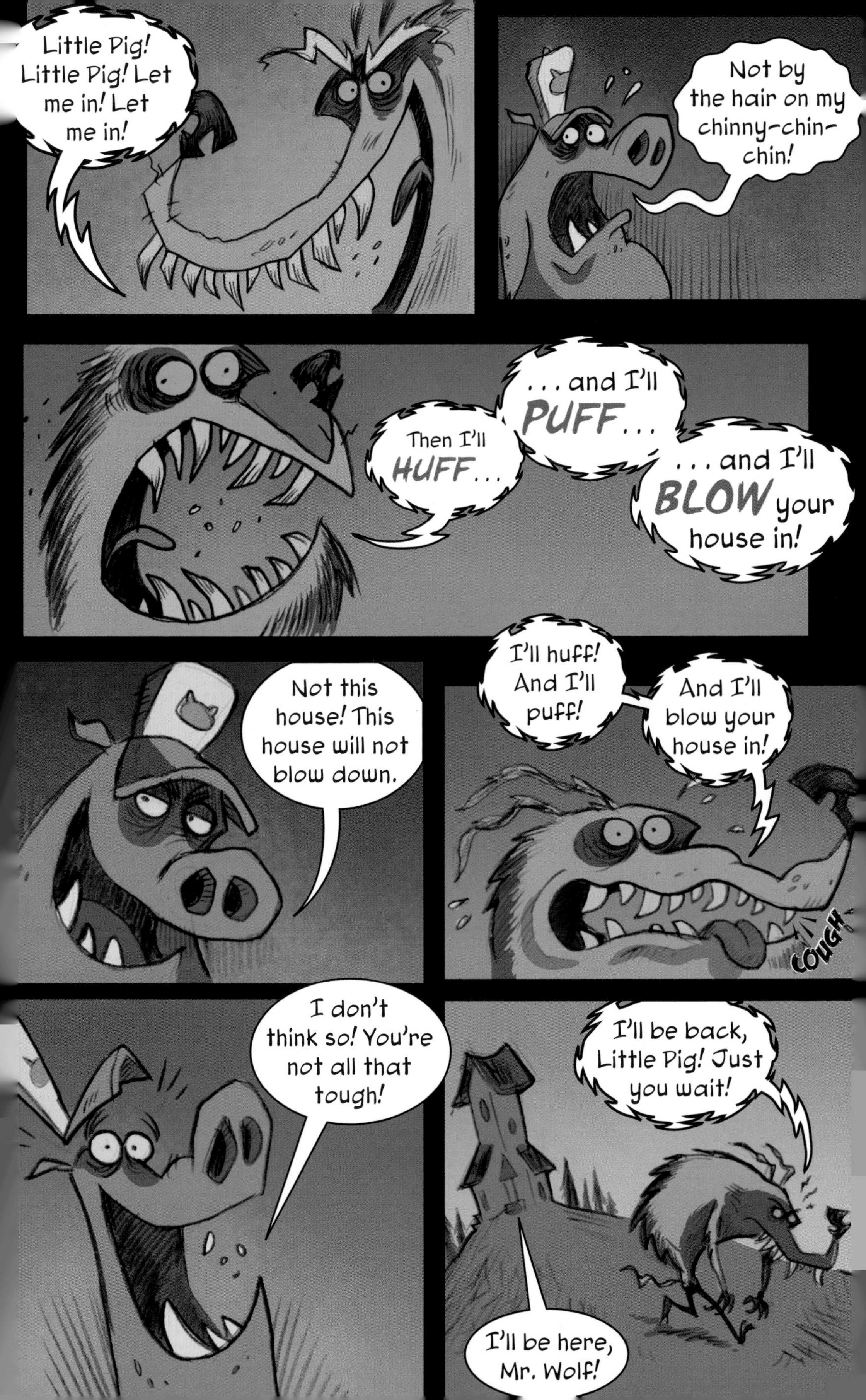
Little Pig! Little Pig! Let me in! Let me in!
Not by the hair on my chinny-chin-chin!
Then I'll HUFF...
...and I'll PUFF...
...and I'll BLOW your house in!
Not this house! This house will not blow down.
I'll huff! And I'll puff!
And I'll blow your house in!
COUGH
I don't think so! You're not all that tough!
I'll be back, Little Pig! Just you wait!
I'll be here, Mr. Wolf!

The next day...

KNOCK KNOCK

#3

Little Pig, I was so rude yesterday. Let me make it up to you.

I know a place where some nice juicy turnips grow.

And where might that be?

At old Farmer Brown's just down the road.

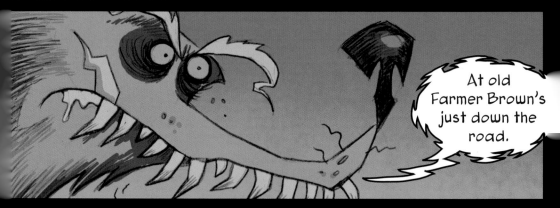

I know the place. Would you like to meet tomorrow morning at six?

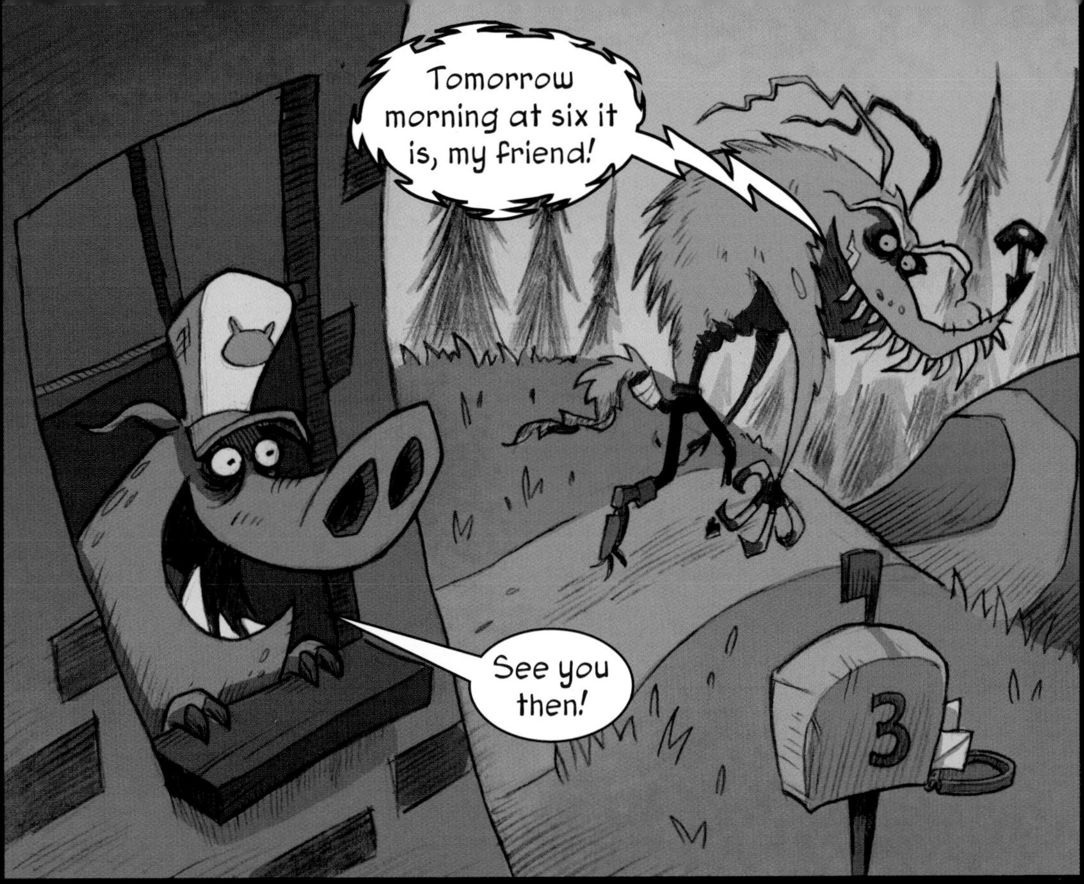
Tomorrow morning at six it is, my friend!
See you then!
3

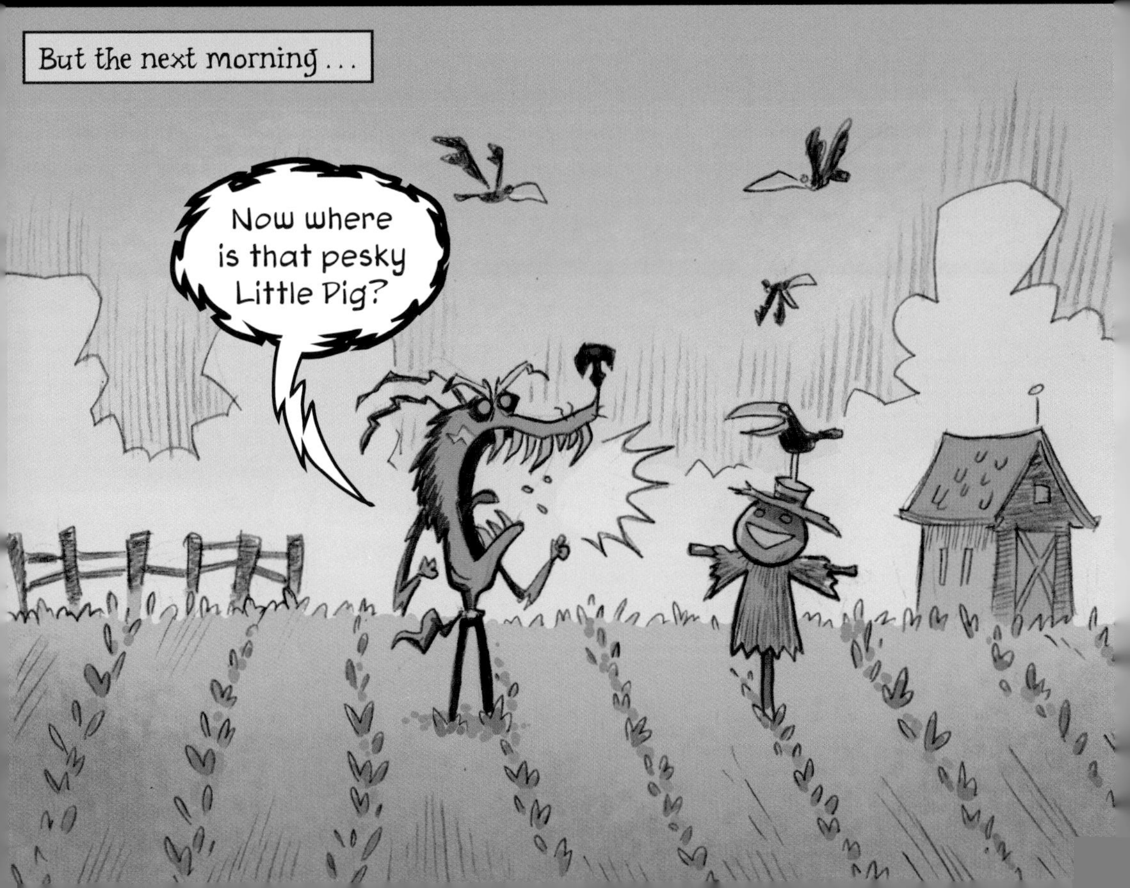
But the next morning . . .
Now where is that pesky Little Pig?

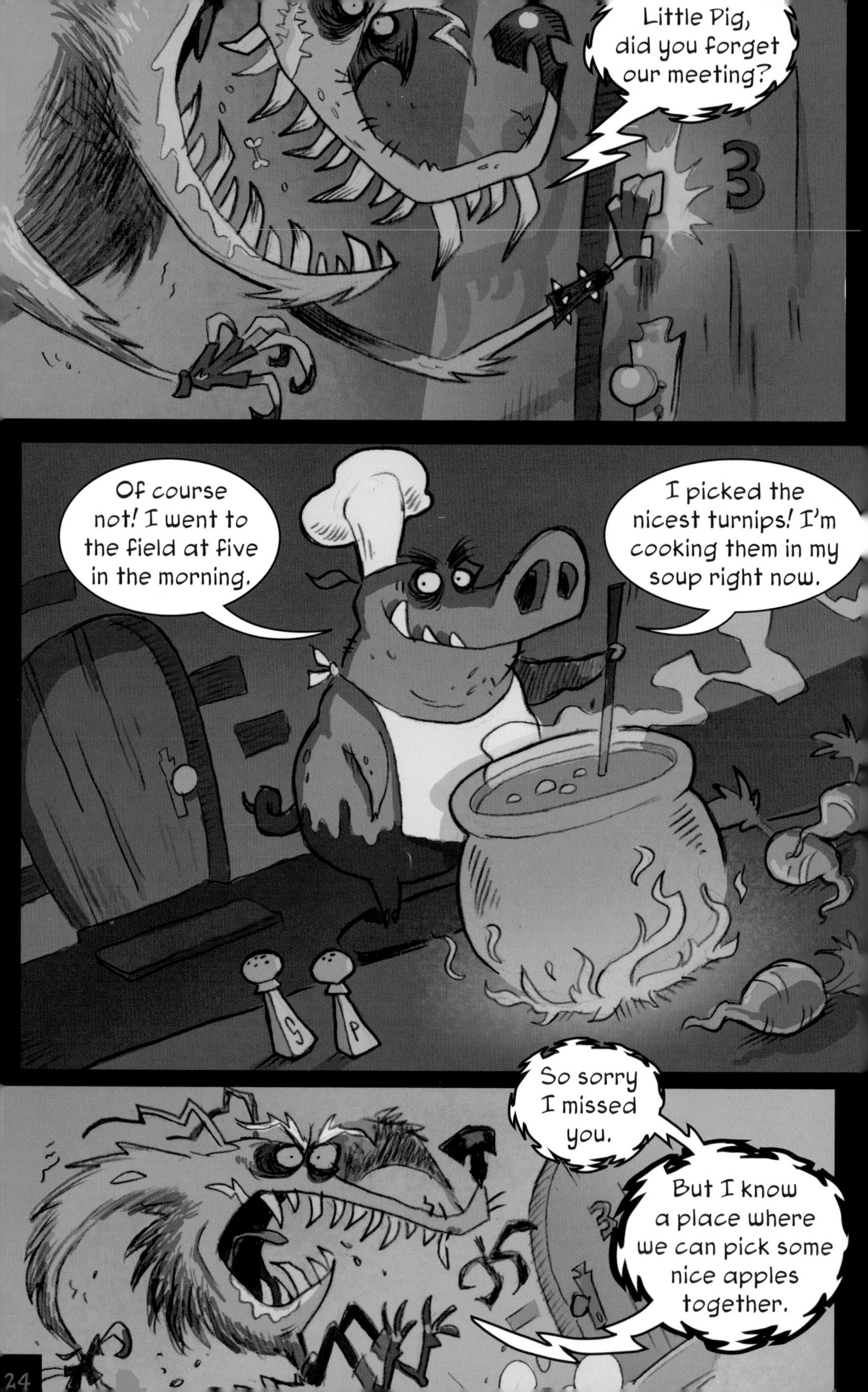
Little Pig, did you forget our meeting?
3
Of course not! I went to the field at five in the morning.
I picked the nicest turnips! I'm cooking them in my soup right now.
S
P
So sorry I missed you.
But I know a place where we can pick some nice apples together.

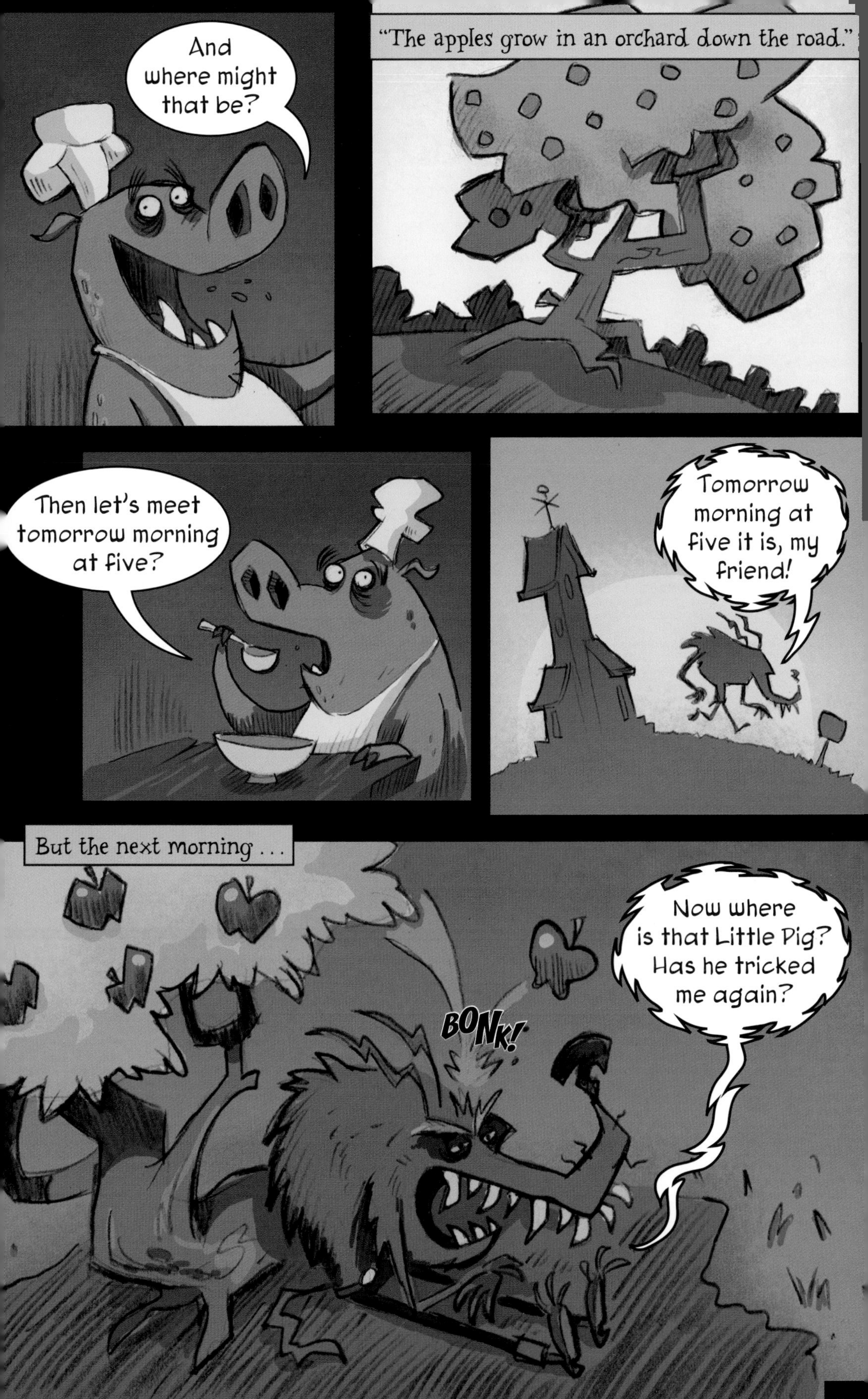

And where might that be?
"The apples grow in an orchard down the road."
Then let's meet tomorrow morning at five?
Tomorrow morning at five it is, my friend!
But the next morning . . .
Now where is that Little Pig? Has he tricked me again?
BONK!

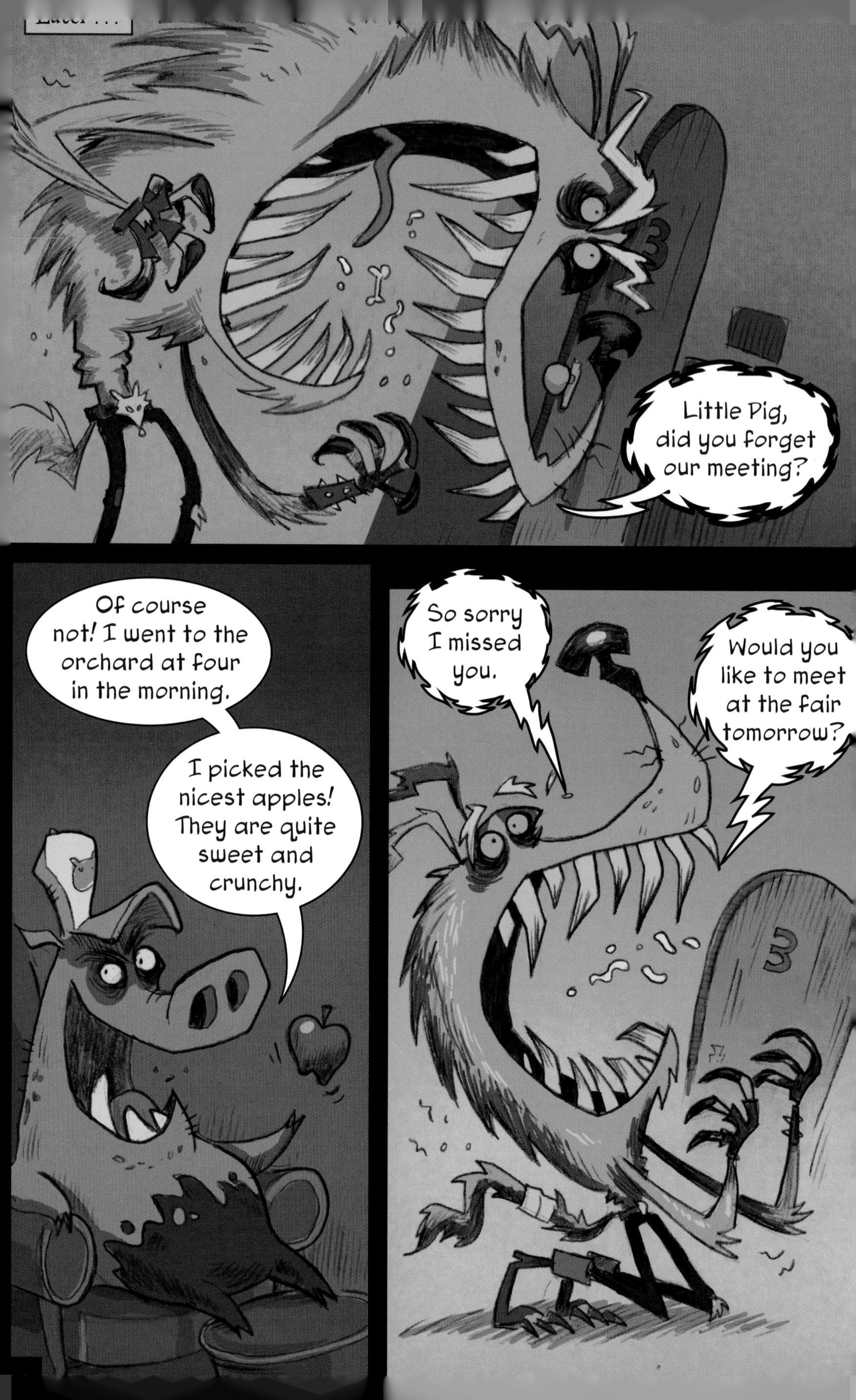
Little Pig, did you forget our meeting?
Of course not! I went to the orchard at four in the morning.
I picked the nicest apples! They are quite sweet and crunchy.
So sorry I missed you.
Would you like to meet at the fair tomorrow?

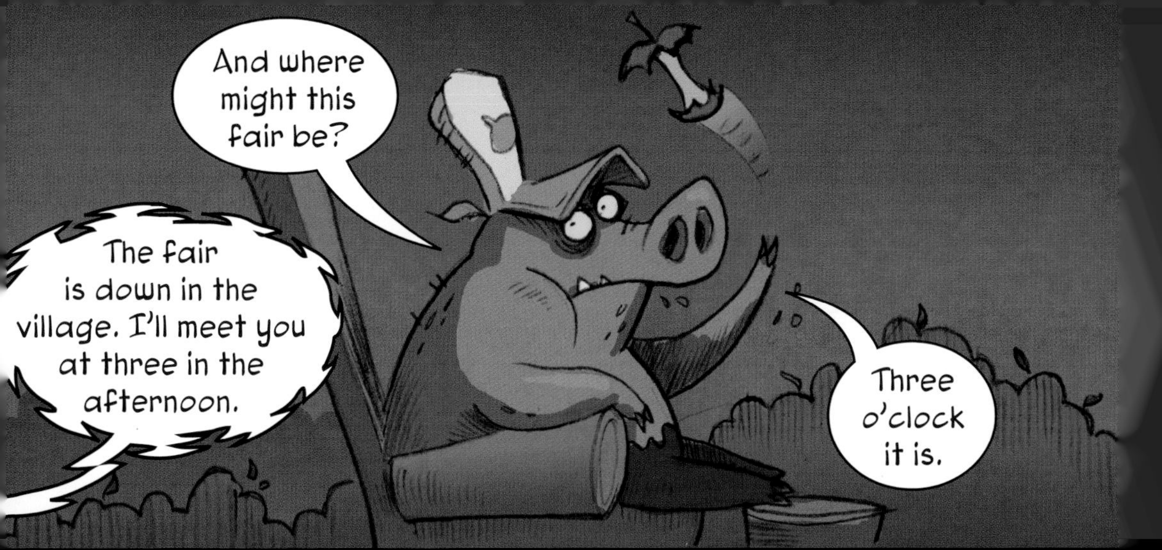
And where might this fair be?
The fair is down in the village. I'll meet you at three in the afternoon.
Three o'clock it is.

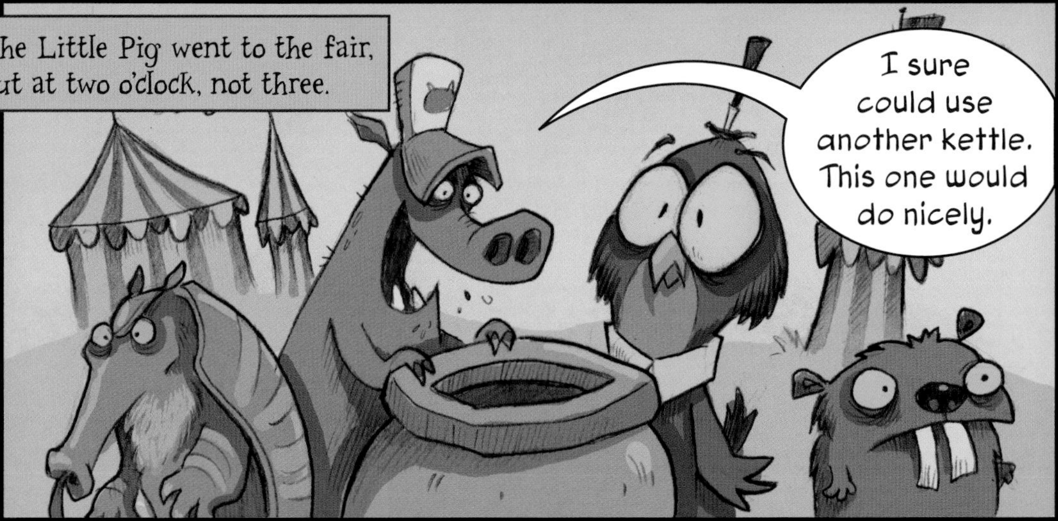
The Little Pig went to the fair, but at two o'clock, not three.
I sure could use another kettle. This one would do nicely.

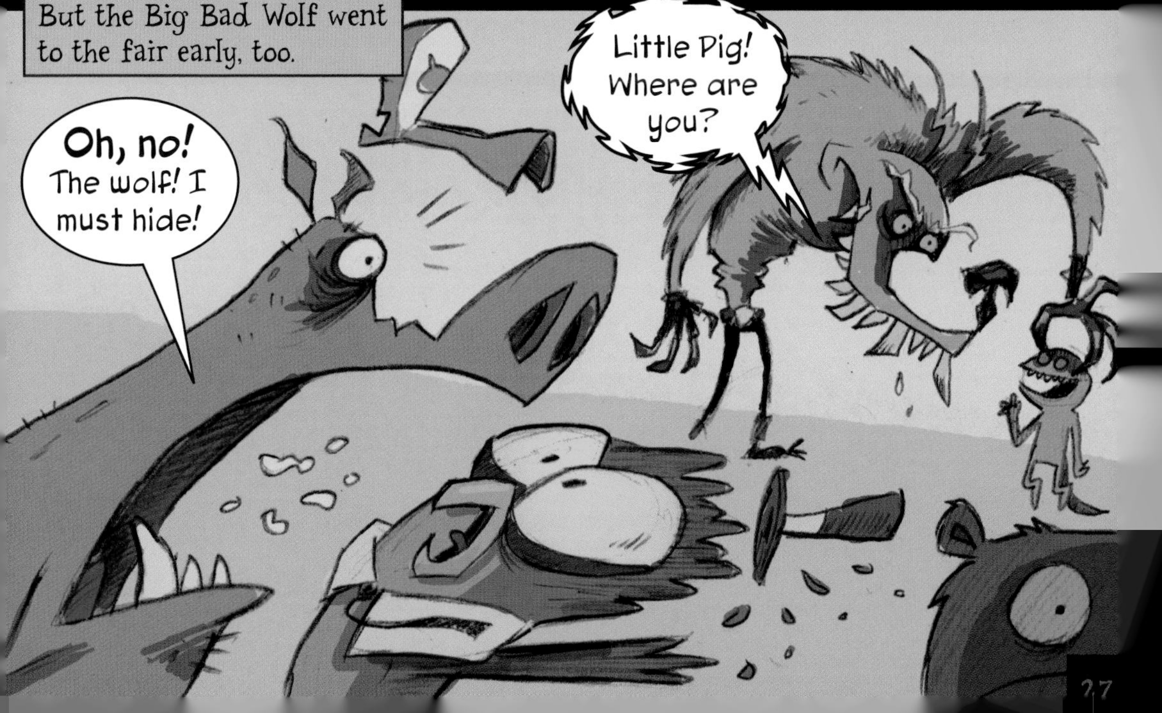
But the Big Bad Wolf went to the fair early, too.
Little Pig! Where are you?
Oh, no! The wolf! I must hide!

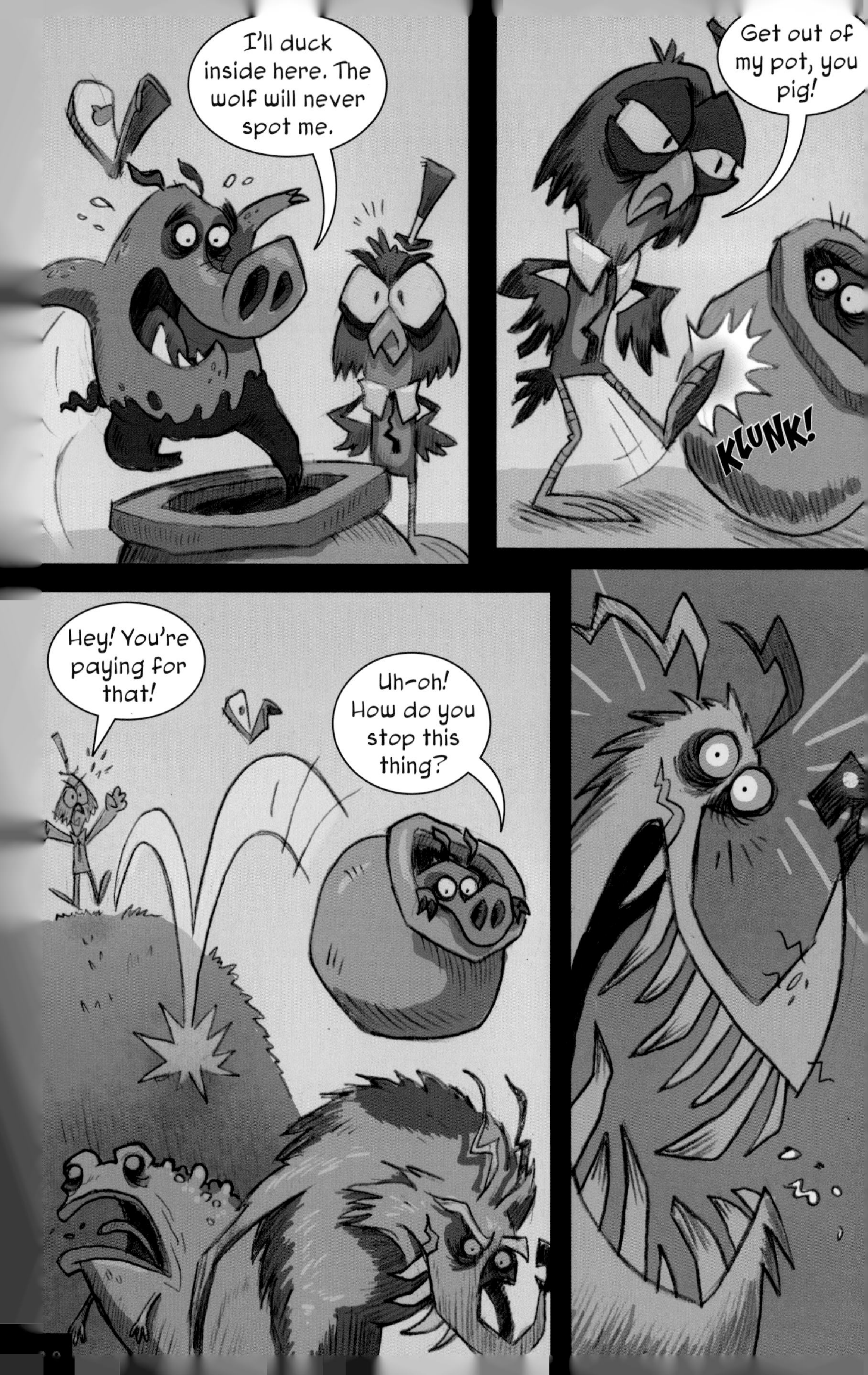
I'll duck inside here. The wolf will never spot me.
Get out of my pot, you pig!
KLUNK!
Hey! You're paying for that!
Uh-oh! How do you stop this thing?

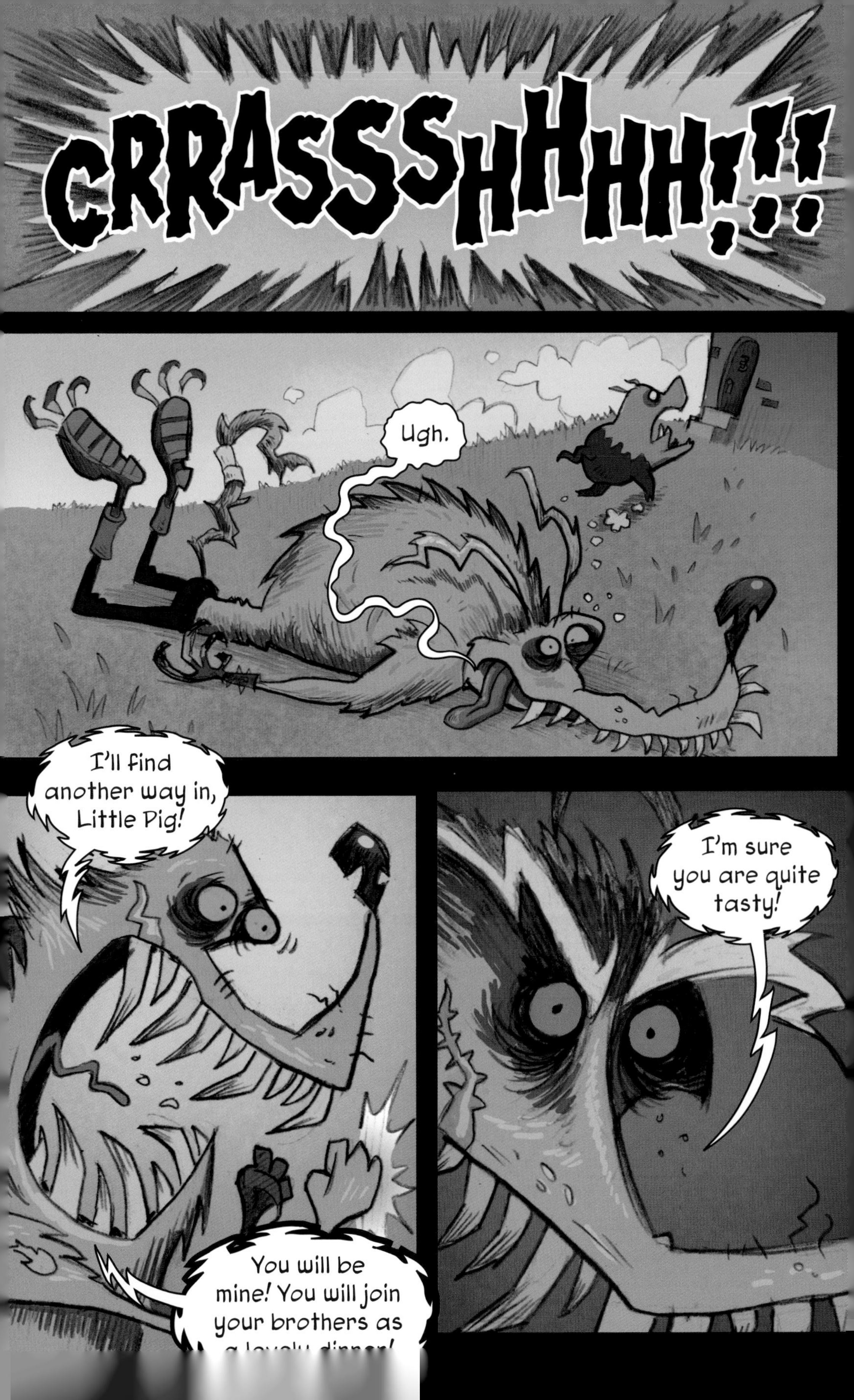
CRRASSSHHHHH!!!
Ugh.
I'll find another way in, Little Pig!
You will be mine! You will join your brothers as
I'm sure you are quite tasty!

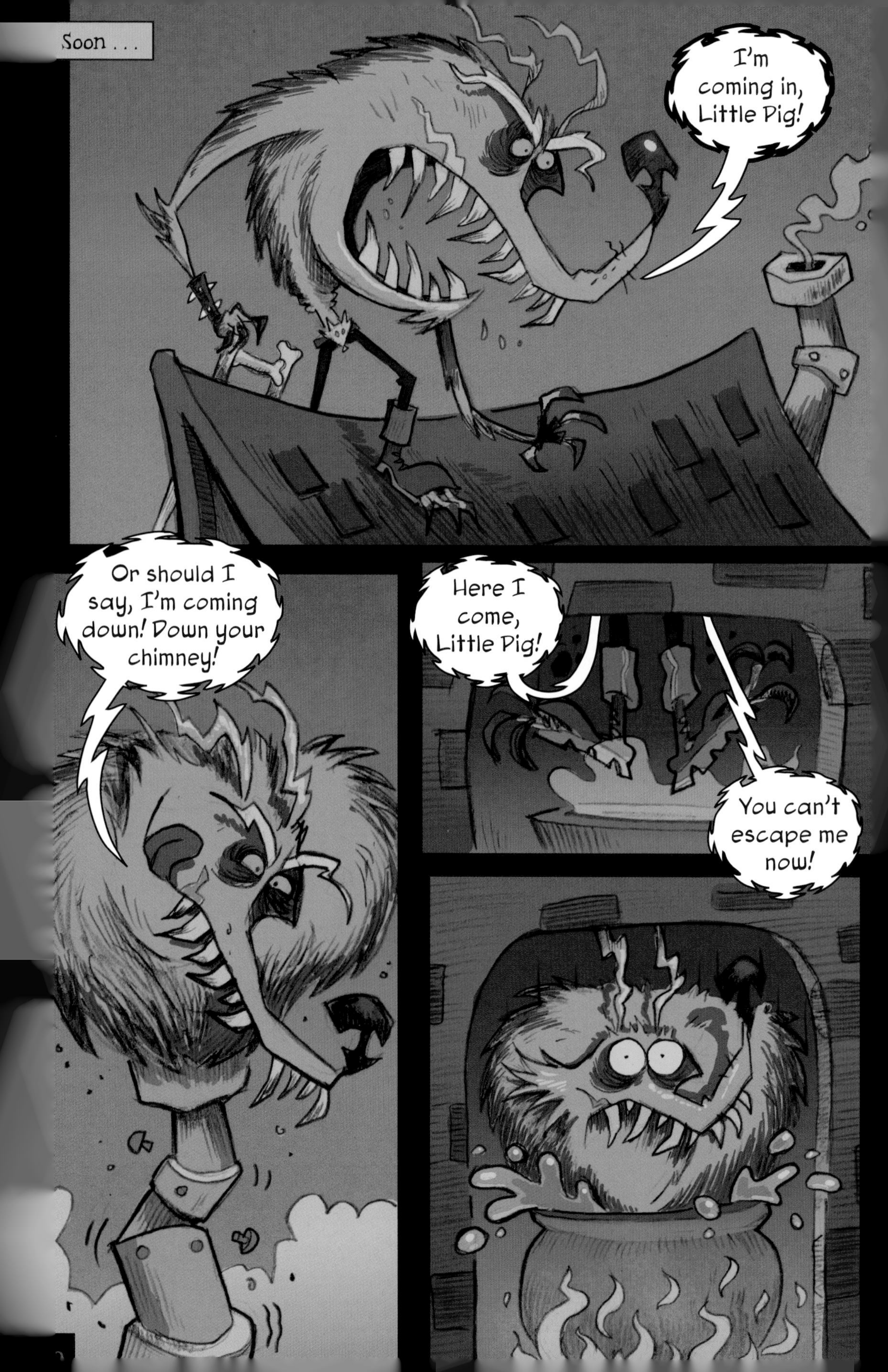
Soon . . .
I'm coming in, Little Pig!
Or should I say, I'm coming down! Down your chimney!
Here I come, Little Pig!
You can't escape me now!

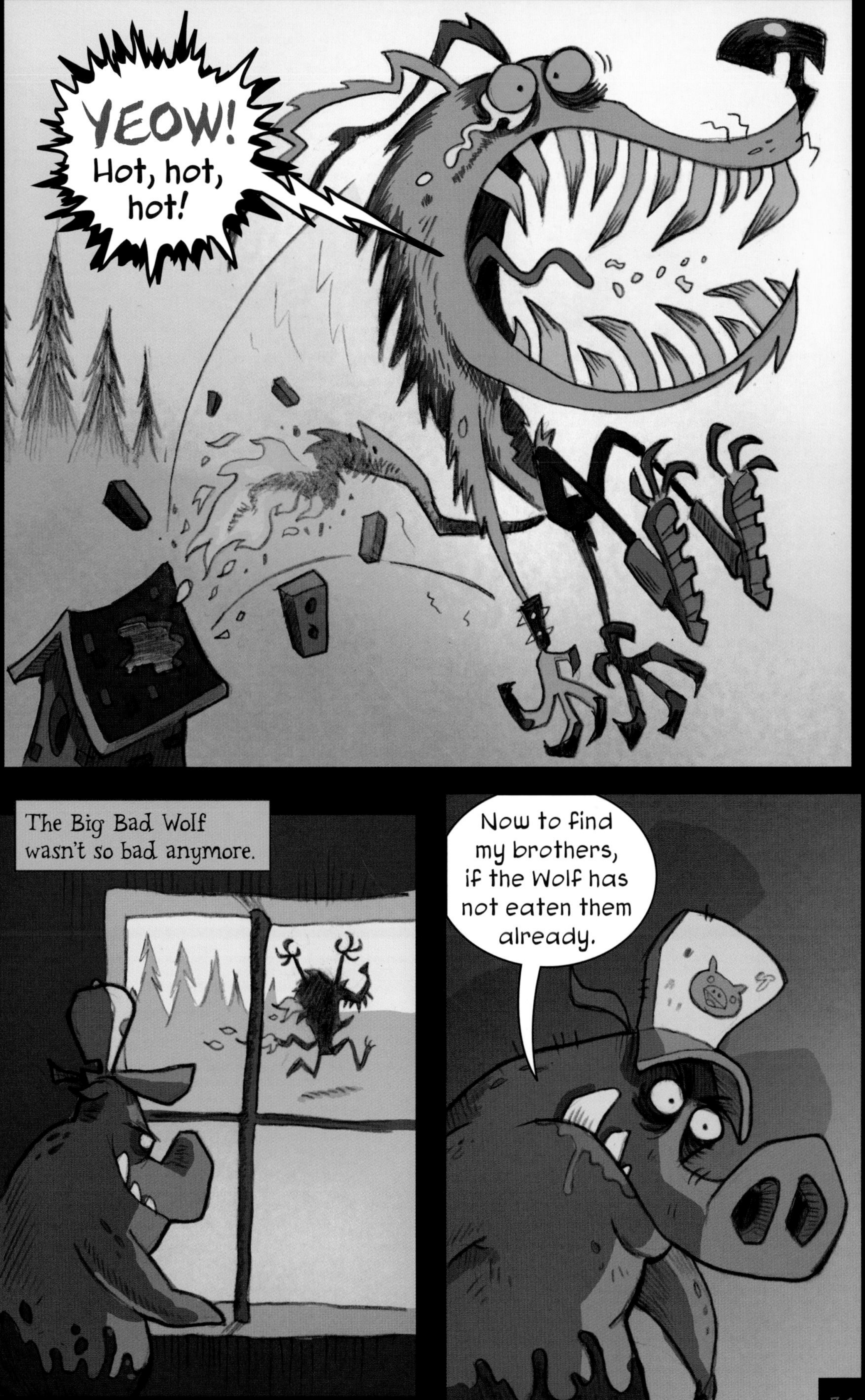
YEOW! Hot, hot, hot!
The Big Bad Wolf wasn't so bad anymore.
Now to find my brothers, if the Wolf has not eaten them already.

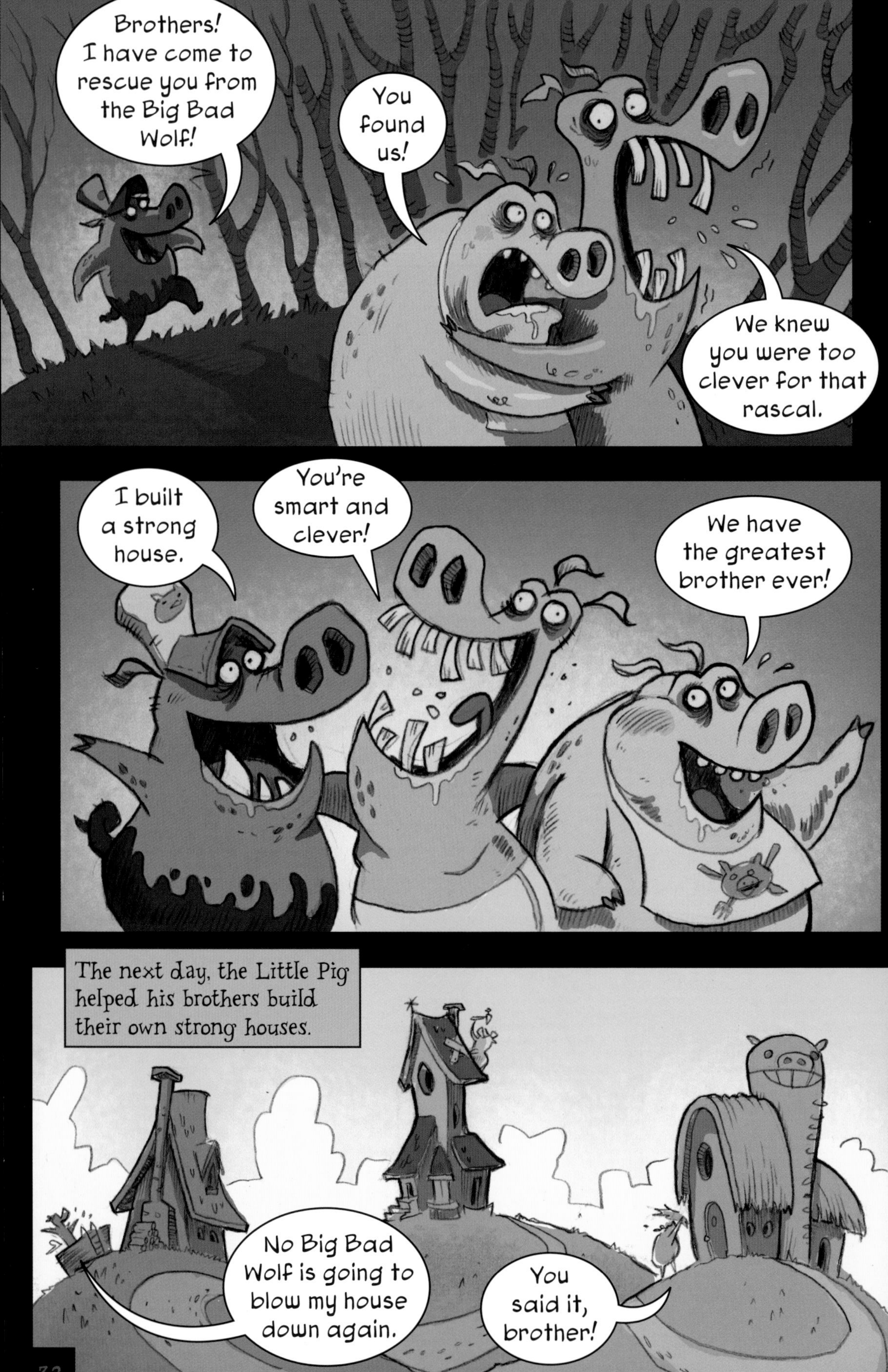
Brothers! I have come to rescue you from the Big Bad Wolf!
You found us!
We knew you were too clever for that rascal.
I built a strong house.
You're smart and clever!
We have the greatest brother ever!
The next day, the Little Pig helped his brothers build their own strong houses.
No Big Bad Wolf is going to blow my house down again.
You said it, brother!

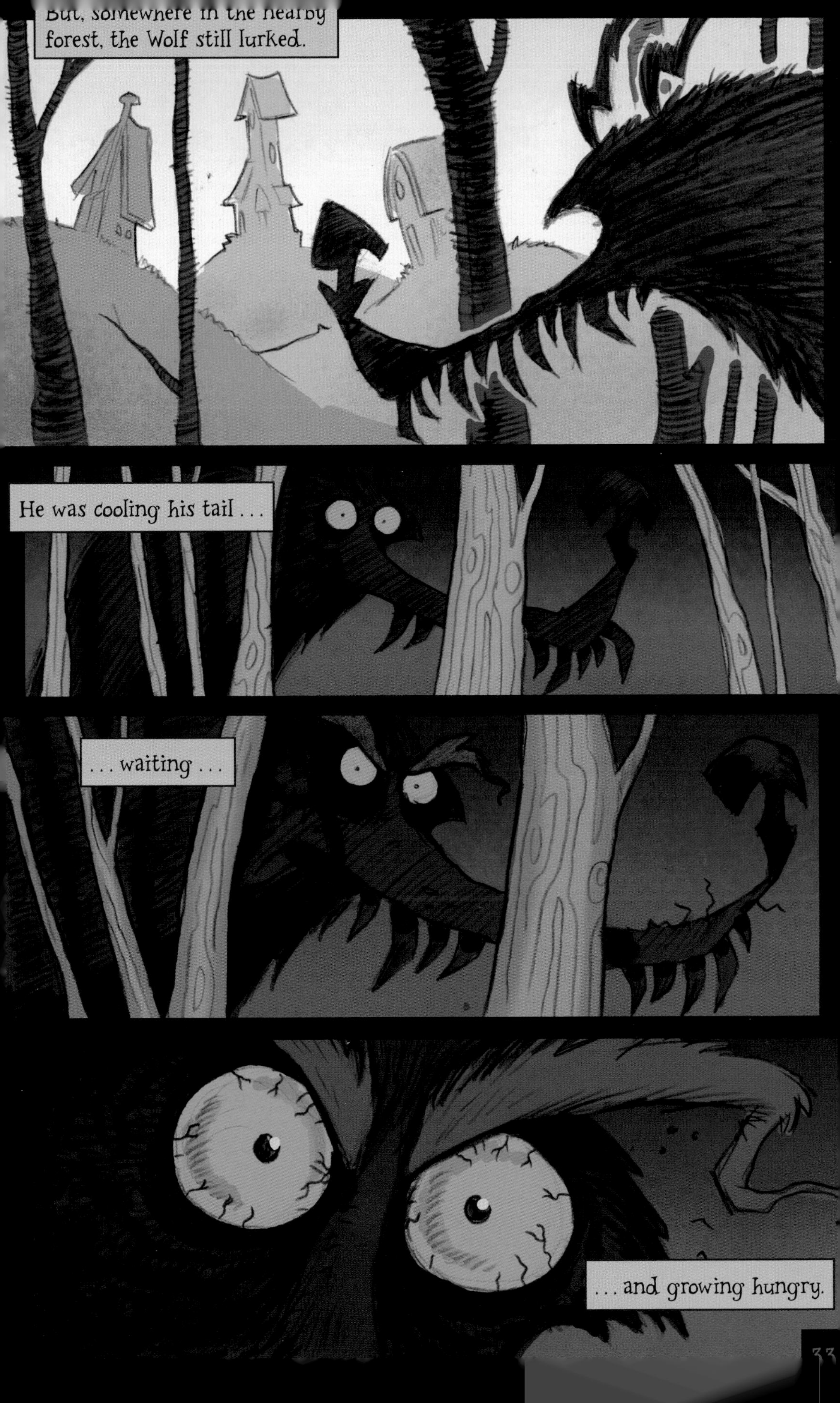
But, somewhere in the nearby forest, the Wolf still lurked.
He was cooling his tail . . .
. . . waiting . . .
. . . and growing hungry.

ABOUT THE AUTHOR

Lisa Trumbauer was the *New York Times* bestselling author of *A Practical Guide to Dragons*. In addition, she wrote about 300 other books for children, including mystery novels, picture books, and nonfiction books on just about every topic under the sun. (Including the sun!)

ABOUT THE ILLUSTRATOR

Aaron Blecha was raised by a school of slimy, yet gooey, giant squids in Green Bay, Wisconsin. Since then, Blecha has been working for ten years as an illustrator and designer with a hodgepodge of fun clients in the animation, publishing, toy, and entertainment industries. After many years in San Francisco, he now resides in London, where he is busy freelancing, avoiding crusty ghosts, and searching for the elusive Squidsquatch.

GLOSSARY

den (DEN)—home of a wild animal

kettle (KET-uhl)—a metal pot used for cooking

orchard (OR-churd)—a field or farm where fruit trees are grown

peddler (PED-lur)—someone who travels around selling things

rascal (RASS-kuhl)—someone who is mischievous or dishonest

rescue (RESS-kyoo)—to save someone who is in danger or trapped somewhere

sturdy (STUR-dee)—strong and firm

tricked (TRIKD)—fooled or cheated someone

turnip (TUR-nuhp)—a round, root vegetable

THE HISTORY OF THE
THREE LITTLE PIGS

Fairy tales are told in every corner of the world. No matter where they come from, there are similar elements in all fairy tales. There are almost always mythical characters, ranging from troublesome trolls to talking animals. Most fairy tales plot the "good" against the "evil," and many teach a lesson.

"The Three Little Pigs" has all of these features. Three house-building pigs battle against the sly wolf. In the end, the pig who took his time and built a proper home out of bricks is the only one to outsmart the wolf.

While the story of the three pigs has likely been around for centuries, it was not published until the 1800s. Writer Joseph Jacobs is credited with the most famous version of the tale. He published it in his collection, *English Fairy Tales,* in 1898. In this early version, the wolf eats the first and second pigs. In turn, the third pig boils up the wolf after he falls in the pot, then eats him for dinner.

Most early-published versions of the tale come from England. However, similar stories can be traced to other countries. "The Three Hares," a Turkish story, tells the tale of three rabbits and a fox. The first rabbit makes his home in a bush, only to be caught and eaten by the fox. The next rabbit tries out tree roots, but the fox eats him too. Finally, the third rabbit digs a long, deep burrow into the ground. Here he is safe from the fox, as well as from dogs and hunters.

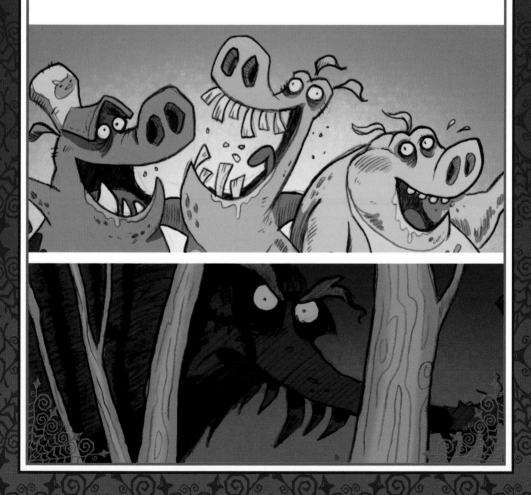

DISCUSSION QUESTIONS

1. Why do you think the first two brothers chose to build their homes with straw and sticks? Why do you think the third brother chose to build with bricks? What might this say about their characters?

2. The story says that the Big Bad Wolf doesn't mean to be nasty, but it was just in his nature. What does that mean? Can you think of other animals that behave a certain way because it is in their "nature"?

3. Each page of a graphic novel has several illustrations inside different panels. What is your favorite panel in this book? Describe what you like about the illustration and why it's your favorite.

WRITING PROMPTS

1. Imagine that the third little pig gets caught too. How could all three of the pigs escape the Big Bad Wolf? Write the getaway story.

2. Write your own version of "The Three Little Pigs," using different animals or even people as the characters. Who will be the hero in the story? Who will be the villain?

3. The wolf used turnips, apples, and the fair to tempt the third little pig out of his home. Pretend you are the little pig. What are three of your favorite things that the wolf might tempt you with?

INTERNET SITES

The book may be over, but the adventure is just beginning.

Do you want to read more about the subjects or ideas in this book? Want to play cool games or watch videos about the authors who write these books? Then go to FactHound. At www.facthound.com, you'll be able to do all that, and more. The FactHound website can also send you to other safe Internet sites.

Check it out!

Date Due